TESSILI
ROGUE

BOOKS BY ROBIN STEPHEN

Chronicles of the Tessilari
Tessili Academy
Tessili Rogue
Tessili Revenge

Annals of the Brinlocks
Brinlin Isle
Brinlin Forest
Brinlin Cove

Tessili Rogue

Chronicles of the Tessilari: Book II

A Story of Bydaira

Robin Stephen

BROWN WING
PRESS

This is a work of fiction. All characters, events, and organization portrayed in this novel are either product's of the author's imagination or are used fictitiously.

TESSILI ROGUE

Copyright © 2015 by Brown Wing Press

robinstephen.com

ISBN 978-0-9844912-6-1 (ebook)
ISBN 978-0-692-51906-6 (print)

Cover design by Robin Deutschendorf
Maps by Robin Deutschendorf

Brown Wing Press
Iowa City, IA
brownwingpress.com

First Brown Wing Press Edition

for my brother, for pushing me to explore new horizons

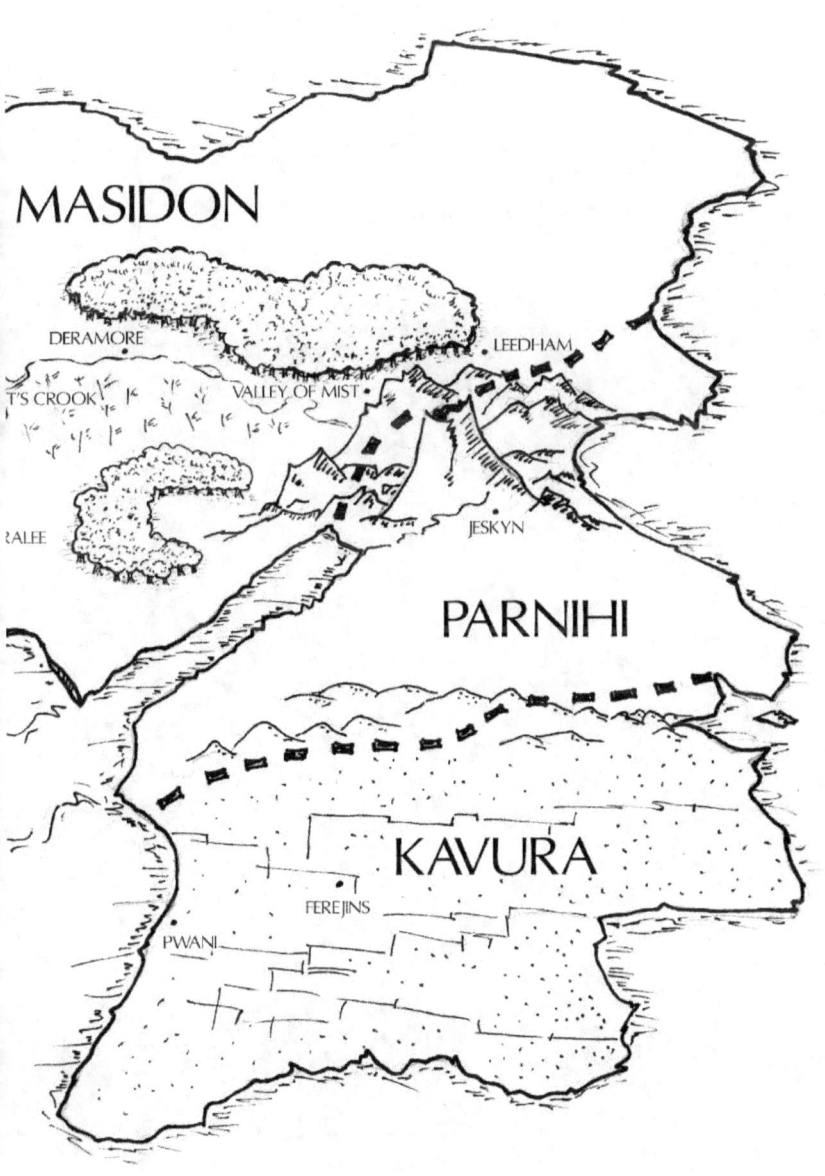

BYDAIRA

MASIDON

DERAMORE

LEEDHAM

VALLEY OF MIST

T'S CROOK

RALEE

JESKYN

PARNIHI

KAVURA

FEREJINS

PWANI

CHAPTER 1

Ever since he'd been a boy, Lokim had wanted to leave the Valley of Mist.

As a child, he'd tested the boundaries. He would make forays into the gray, swirling fog that encircled the valley. He'd keep going as his vision went soft, until the air grew muffled and chill. As the world faded from view his heart would begin to pound with fear. He would turn back when he was one step away from losing his memory of which direction led home.

When he'd been older, he'd made a more serious attempt. One bright day he'd slipped into the fog and begun to walk. He'd moved ahead with determination, going further than he'd ever gone before. He'd walked and walked, certain with every step he'd make it, that the air would clear and he'd see … he'd see the world.

Except, he hadn't. After marching forward for an hour, he'd thought the fog seemed thinner. He'd hurried ahead, eyes, straining, only to find himself emerging from the mists in the precise spot he'd entered them.

High Mage Agina had been waiting for him, eyes flinty, firm mouth set in a hard line.

Lokim had known better than to try again.

For a time, he'd given up. He'd contented himself with watching for rovers. Every time a group came in from their travels, he would ask for stories. Most of them developed a sort of annoyed fondness for the boy. They would answer questions if they had nothing better to do. But the rovers never stayed for long.

When, years later, Lokim had his moment and succeeded in passing beyond the veil, he'd thought himself prepared. He'd mastered the skills the rovers said he would need to survive. He thought he understood the ways of the people he would find beyond the veil. Like all the Tessilari, he'd studied the histories. He knew about the Betrayal and all that had followed.

He'd been prepared to find monsters. What he'd discovered was people.

◈

Shai was not happy. Jey could feel his rage, boiling out of the tessila's small body like dull heat, filling her with the desire to let him go.

Jey was ignoring him. Or, at least, she was trying to. It wasn't easy. The small creature lay within the grip of her left hand, delicate wings pinned to his small body, purple head protruding from between her index finger and thumb, tail lashing beyond her pinkie. Unlike Phril, Shai had a set of sharp spikes along the base of his skull. Jey's hand now bled where he'd used these to stab her. It was tricky, holding him tight enough to prevent his escape, but not so tight as to do him any harm.

Phril was also not happy. He did not like Jey to have contact with any tessila other than himself. He crouched on her wrist a few inches away from Shai. He was coiled into an angry knot, wings flared, hissing at the other tessila every time he stabbed Jey with the spikes.

Jey was trying to read. Holdam had loaned her a text on the methods of preparing soft cheeses. It was an old book, well worn, with many of Holdam's own notes written in the margins.

After her long day working in the cheesery, Jey was exhausted. It was well past midnight. She glanced with longing at the two tidy beds that stood on the other side of the small room. They were both neatly made, plain woolen blankets tucked in, down pillows fluffed. *I could lie down for just a moment.*

Jey squashed the thought. She knew better than to give in to fatigue. Her duty was to hold Shai. Shai did not want to be held. It would take only a moment of carelessness for him to escape her grasp. And that would be a disaster.

Jey rubbed her forehead with her free hand. She moved her small dish of oil with its wick and flame closer to the book. The spidery handwriting on the page seemed to swim before her eyes.

There was a tap on the chamber door.

Jey jerked in her seat, resisting the impulse to fling Shai from her hand, launch herself across the room, and draw the two long knives from where they lay hidden beneath her mattress. She spat out a quiet curse, cast two quick passive echo spells—one on Phril, one on Shai—instructed Phril to hold still so the spell would actually work, and said in a mild tone, "Come in."

Jey turned in her chair. Her heart was pounding. Her desire to arm herself grew intolerably intense as the latch clicked and the door swung inward, spilling a little more light into the dim room.

Biala poked her head around the door. Her long braid, shot with gray, hung down before one shoulder. Her expression, lit by the candle she held, was friendly. She looked into the room. "I saw your light. I admire your thirst for knowledge, Jey, but you young people should not neglect your rest."

Jey blinked in what she hoped looked like abstracted bemusement, gazing at the inky night outside the window. "I didn't realize it had grown so late."

But Biala's brow had furrowed as she took in the rest of the room. Her mouth compressed into a small frown. "But where is Elle?"

Jey felt fatigue bloom through her as Shai increased his squirming in a sudden renewed bid for freedom. She was so tired. If she couldn't talk her way out of this, she'd have to cast a passive persuasion spell on Biala. Passive persuasions were Elle's specialty, not hers. It was the last thing she needed.

Jey stood, easing out of her chair and moving a few steps closer to the woman and her candle. She tried to do so in a way that suggested nothing more than a desire to stretch her legs. "She couldn't sleep, so she went for a walk." She made her tone mild and lazy, as if it was the most normal thing in the world for an 18 year old girl to wander outside, alone, at night, in the dead of winter.

Biala's eyes narrowed further. "A walk?" she said. "At midnight?"

Jey was about the answer, but a sudden stab of pain in her hand caused her to almost cry out. Shai had flung his head against her hand with the greatest force he'd managed yet. The spikes on the back of his head bit into the base of her index finger. Phril, stirred to anger, leapt forward. He would have attacked the other tessila had Jey not cupped her free hand over Shai to protect him. Shai proceeded to pull his spikes free and drive them in again.

Something of her pain and distraction must have shown on Jey's face, because Biala's eyes softened. She let out a small chuckle, looking again at Jey, the oil light, the book, the two empty beds. She winked and turned, leaving the astonished Jey to stare at her back. "Delari knows, there's nothing like a full moon to inspire a late night rendezvous. I wonder who the lucky young man is."

Jey didn't answer, and Biala withdrew behind the door. "See you both tomorrow," the woman said. "But warn Elle there will be no lessening of duties for those who choose romance over sleep."

Jey, heart pounding, stood still until the latch clicked. Then she dropped the passive echo spells and glared down at Phril, who was trying to claw his way past her protective hand to get at Shai. "Stop it," she hissed. "Phril. That is enough." She made no attempt to shield him from the frustration and annoyance she was feeling.

Phril, suddenly sulky, flew across the room to alight on the windowsill, seething with resentment. Jey removed her protective hand and looked down at Shai, who was glaring up at her, his sharp face smeared with her blood. Jey sank back into her chair. "Both of you need to calm down. You should know the drill by now."

But they did not know the drill. Tessili were famous for their intractability, but it seemed to Jey both Shai and Phril had been increasingly volatile lately.

She knew Phril was, in part, reacting to her own stress. The truth was, Jey hated these nights – the nights Elle crept off through the darkness to break into Tessili Academy.

◈

Lokim tracked the girl with relative ease. Though she moved through the night with the grace and silence of a hunting cat, Lokim had gotten used to her ways. He knew the way she walked, the places she stopped to watch for pursuit, even the signature of her magic. For the last six months, he'd followed her every time she left the cheesery.

For the last six months, time after time, he'd tried to gather the courage to approach her. But he never had.

The girl, Elle, she was called, paused before stepping into the shallow stream. She would now walk in it for a time, making it more difficult for the hounds to follow her scent. He winced as he watched her step into the cold water. The night was bitter. Shards of ice had formed along the edges of the stream. Elle waded along, her dark leathers soaking up the chill water. Lokim waited until she was all but lost in the darkness before hopping to the other side, keeping his own feet dry.

About a hundred yards down the stream an old, gnarled tree grew above the water. Elle paused and jumped, grabbing a long branch with her gloved hands. She dangled for a moment, then pulled herself up. She moved along the branch and down the trunk. Feet once more on the ground, she broke into a steady jog, heading towards the outskirts of Deramor and the cheesery where she now lived.

Lokim let out an admiring breath. He'd never seen anyone so graceful, so smooth, so slender and yet so strong. This was one of several spots Elle and Jey used the stream to confuse the dogs and throw them off the trail. So far, it had always worked.

Lokim waited until Elle was almost out of sight. He was about to move again, to follow, when he saw something. It was a faint blur, a shifting in the shadows at the corner of his eye.

He froze, listening. The flowing of the cold stream was a silver chuckle in the still night. He waited.

Another girl emerged from the darkness. She, too, moved with the intent grace of a predator. But unlike Elle, she was not familiar to him. Although Lokim had never seen her before, she wore the same dark leathers as Elle, the same twin knives strapped to her hips. She did not wet her feet, but hopped the stream and paused for a moment, listening.

Lokim's hand flew to the knife on his belt, but the girl was intent on one thing. She continued, tracking Elle as surely as Lokim was.

As the girl disappeared into the dark woods, Bliz swept in a sudden, agitated loop around Lokim's head.

Lokim held out a hand and the orange tessila alighted. He ran a finger along the sharp edge of her chin. "Shush, brilliant one. It's ok." He said these words in the barest of whispers as he began to move, tracking the girl who tracked Elle.

What did it mean? Lokim had developed some theories in the last months, but he had no answers. He didn't know why Jey and Elle returned to a place they appeared to loath, time after time, but he had his guesses. Now, it appeared, their visits had been noticed.

Around him, the woodland that stretched between the walled island and the outlying settlements of the country's capital was empty and silent. For six months, Lokim had told himself he would make contact, he would talk to them. Tomorrow.

But now it seemed tomorrow might be too late.

As Lokim walked, tracking the ghost of the movement that was the second girl, he seemed to hear High Mage Agina's voice, speaking in his head. *Do not trust your ally. He will betray you. Allies are more dangerous than enemies, for they wear a false face. The only true bond is blood.*

These words had held him immobile for six months. They'd held him back, kept him cowering in the shadows, waiting, watching, hoping for some way to know if it was safe to reveal himself. He didn't know if these girls would turn out to be allies or enemies, or a little bit of both.

Now, he realized with a sudden sense of clarity, revealing himself would never be safe. Nothing he'd done since he'd left the Valley of the Mist was safe. But that did not mean it wasn't worth doing.

In the darkness, Lokim drew his knife.

When the door to the chamber opened and Elle slipped into the room, Jey turned, released a long, slow breath, and opened her hand. Shai leapt free, beating his wings to streak towards Elle with a sharp, resentful hiss. Jey left her chair and went to the basin by the window where she dabbed at her bloodied hand with a damp cloth.

Elle closed the door and stepped into the room. She was dressed in the leather clothing they'd stolen from the academy when they'd escaped six months before. Her feet were wet. Her lips were blue with cold, but she reached inside her cloak and drew out a bundle, which she stowed in the back of the trunk where she kept her things. "How much were you able to get?" Jey said.

Elle straightened, sat, and began to unlace her boots. "Quite a lot." She sounded cheerful, even as she grimaced and flicked ice off one of her laces. "The hounds weren't out tonight. I could move freely."

Jey frowned, rinsed the cloth, and dabbed at her punctured hand some more. Elle seemed to register what Jey was doing. She looked down at the blood-smeared Shai, who was clinging to the cuff of one of her gloves.

"Shai. Why must you fight so? You know you'd die if you tried to come with me."

The purple tessila hissed again. Elle sighed and began to try to wipe the blood from the spikes of his skull. "You're a barbarian." Her tone was one of gentle recrimination.

But it wasn't Shai's fault. No tessila could be caged. If a bonded tessila was trapped without his human, he would bludgeon himself against bars or windows, never ceasing his struggle until he had either escaped or died.

Jey wiped her hand dry and turned towards her bed with a feeling of anticipation. She'd taken one step towards it when there was another tap on the door. She froze, more annoyed than afraid this time. "It's Biala," she whispered. "She came by earlier and noticed you were gone."

Elle, who had uncoiled her dark braid from where it had been pinned up at the back of her head, looked down at her leathers in sudden consternation. "I can't change in time," she said. "I'll have to fudge her memory."

Jey frowned. Elle was much better at passive persuasion spells than Jey was. She was responsible for the fact Biala and Holdam had welcomed them into their home, accepting their story about being sent by an uncle who was an old friend who'd set things up so they could work here in exchange for room and board. Elle had been deft about it, and minimal. It had taken only a small amount of reinforcement here or there to keep the older couple from realizing they didn't have a friend who met the description of Elle and Jey's fictional uncle, or from showing too much curiosity about the girls and their past lives.

Even though Elle was good, Jey regretted the necessity of using passive persuasion on anybody, particularly these people who were kind and trusting and fair. Jey liked to keep the magical meddling to an absolute minimum.

But Elle was right. There was no time. She gave an unhappy nod. She said, for the second time that night, "Come in."

The latch clicked instantly, as if someone had been standing with a hand on the knob. The door opened on a dark, empty hallway. There was the quiet shush of moving air. The door closed as if of its own accord.

Jey stared at the seemingly empty place before the door, her heart beginning to pound as the implications sank in. With a small cry of surprise, she dove towards the bed and her knives.

A voice, male and low, sounded in the flame lit dimness of their chamber. "I come in peace. Please, I beg you. Let me speak."

Jey reached the bed, groped below the mattress, and straightened. Feeling better now the smooth wooden grips of her knives rested in her hands, she turned and focused on the spot the man's voice had come from. She prepared to throw.

Then, slowly, a shape materialized on the air above the desk. It was a flitting shadow at first, nothing more remarkable than a falling leaf. The shape resolved into a tessila – brilliant scales dancing orange in the light of the single flame. Phril turned from his position on the windowsill, glittering eyes intent. Shai flared his wings and let out a long, low cry of greeting.

The voice spoke again. "I am not a threat. See? I am like you."

As the two girls stared at the looping flight of the orange tessila, the air next to the desk began to shimmer as well. An outline appeared first, then filled in with detail.

A man stood there – young and tall and straight.

As he regarded them with his dark, earnest eyes, Jey remembered where she'd seen him before.

"My name is Lokim," he said. "And there's something I need to show you."

CHAPTER 2

The moon was beginning to set when Jey and Elle hurried through the small wooden fence that opened from the side of the cheesery's yard onto the cobbled street. The two girls moved swiftly, wrapped in dark cloaks. Elle had put on dry socks and shoved her feet back into her boots. The strange man had said he would meet them at the place where the north lane led into the woods as soon as they could arrive. Then he'd vanished again, gone from the room as suddenly as he'd entered.

After a brief, intense conversation, Elle and Jey had decided they had no choice but to make the rendezvous. Since leaving the academy, they had not seen a single tessila other than their own. But this man had one, which meant he knew things Jey and Elle needed to find out.

Jey had strapped on her gear belt. Elle had loaded her crossbow. They'd left, their tessili darting on the air overhead.

Now, as they hurried through the quiet streets of Deramor, a thousand questions bit at Jey's mind. Who was this man? How had he known where to find them? As she walked, she rubbed the heel of one hand over her right forearm where the strange, blue-tinted magical gash had marked her arm months before. That wound had been the tipping point – the beginning of the crazy spiral of events that had led Jey, Elle, and Kae to escape from the academy, and Kae to lose her life when her tessila was killed in the process.

"He's the one who attacked me," she whispered to Elle as they passed the few other homes of craftsmen between the cheesery and the road. "Months ago, when I was on an opportunity."

Elle, moving as silently as smoke, said, "I thought you attacked him?"

Jey grimaced and shrugged. Before she could answer the road wound past the last building. Trees began to rear up on either side of them. Phril, elated to be out, flitted and danced in the frigid air. He did not like the cold, but for now his excitement and curiosity kept him from noticing the temperature.

"Here." The voice came from off the road. Jey turned to see the strange young man step out from behind a tree long enough for them to see him. Then he stepped out of sight again.

Nervous now, Jey drew her knives. It seemed an odd way to set a trap, but she and Elle hadn't stayed free by growing careless. Jey went first, knives bared. Elle came behind, short, brutal crossbow held at ready.

Jey moved up an incline and around a tree. She looked down into a moonlit vale.

Lokim was there, crouching on the ground next to a slender girl. She was bound and gagged and lay in the pool of her dark cloak.

It was a cloak exactly like the one Jey wore now, and Elle also.

The girl was a student at the academy.

Jey hurried forward, sheathing her knives as she moved down the incline. When Jey stopped at the girl's feet, Elle moved ahead. She crouched, touching a dark discoloration on the girl's forehead. "I hit her," Lokim said. He sounded embarrassed. "With the hilt of my knife. She was following you, Elle. When you stopped at the edge of town to make sure no one was about, I hit her and tied her up."

Jey and Elle stared at each other. A bitter wind stirred their cloaks. Phril came and darted above the girl's head. The man's orange tessila joined him. For a moment the two flitting shapes were a blur of movement in the silver air.

"What are we going to do with her?" Elle said. She straightened from her examination of the girl's wound. "I think she'll wake up soon. If we let her go, she'll go back and tell them … she'll tell them she saw us, that I came here to Deramor."

Jey felt dread uncoil in her heart. The man, only a shadow, watched them with unconcealed interest. His eyes were dark and intense in the low light. She ignored him, focusing on the more immediate problem. She spoke to Elle. "Can you fudge her memory?"

Elle shook her head with uncertainty. "The flashnodes," she said. "The drugs. It's too many unknowns. I could try, but I don't know if it would hold."

The dread grew sharper. Jey looked down at the slender girl. She lay with her eyes closed. Her hair was coiled and pinned, the same way Jey's own orderly had taught her to pin hers up years ago. Her skin was covered by dark leather, but Jey knew if she could see the inside of the girl's left arm she'd find it pocked and scarred by the pricks of dozens of needles. On her wrist a plain silver bracelet gleamed. Jey felt giddy with rage at the sight of it. She remembered the oath she had been forced to speak each time she was sent on an opportunity. *Once I have left this place, I will not pursue any other task, desire, or goal other than that which I have been given until I have returned.* She remembered the searing pain it had caused Phril each time she'd tested the oath and tried to defy her orders.

Elle seemed to be following Jey's train of thought. She spoke in a desolate tone. "It's not her fault, what she is. She's like we were."

The three of them were silent a long while. Jey said nothing. She could think of a dozen ways to quickly and painlessly kill this girl without waking her. Jey, after all, had been trained since her earliest days, honed into a lethal weapon. Jey had killed many people in her life, including sleeping girls not so different from this one.

But that had been before. Before she'd had any choice.

Elle, eyes desperate, looked at Jey. "We can't kill her."

Jey closed her eyes. She was certain she'd never been so tired in her life. For six months they'd been dodging the hounds and the trackers the academy sent looking for them. They'd barely made it through those first desperate weeks as they'd tried to form a plan, to come up with a sustainable way to move forward. Winter had forced them out of the woods and into the cheesery, but still they were not independent. They needed brillbane seed sacks if their tessili were going to survive. And in spite of searching every inch of the woods surrounding

Deramor, they had not found a single wild brillbane plant.

Lokim cleared his throat. He spoke into the silence of the night, his words slow and somber. "There might be another way," he said. "If you were willing to leave this place, I could offer you the protection of my people."

Lokim waited as the girls withdrew to discuss his offer. It was hard, letting them move away. More than anything, he was afraid of spooking them – afraid they would bolt into the shivering night and disappear forever. He didn't doubt they could lose him. He'd been watching them long enough to know they had evasion down to a science. The two girls had different strengths and they worked together seamlessly. Lokim himself had his fair share of skills and abilities. But in the night, in the cold, he doubted he could keep a lock on them if they decided to run.

He waited, trying not to shiver. Bliz came to him and alighted on his collar, worming her way down between the soft fabric and the warm skin of his neck. He could feel the cold in her wings and the excited beating of her heart. She'd been lonely this last year. The tessili bound to the two girls were the first she'd seen since they'd left the Valley of Mist. Now, after her quick flight with Jey's red tessila, Bliz was feeling suddenly shy.

Lokim could not hear what Elle and Jey were saying, but he could follow the undercurrent of their conversation. They were of different minds about what to do.

At last, they seemed to reach an agreement. Jey stepped forward, skirting the bound girl who lay on her cloak. Elle trailed behind, crouching again to set a hand on the girl's temple. "We're going to try a passive persuasion," she said, "and send her back to the academy."

Lokim felt a dip of disappointment, but Jey wasn't done. "At the very least that will give us some time. Even if she does remember, they will still need to search. We've hidden from them before. We can do it again. And maybe she won't remember at all."

Lokim felt a tug on the air as Elle began to weave a spell. He felt it flow out of her slender hands, settling, sinking into the unconscious girl's mind. "She's very good at passive persuasion," Jey added.

The girl on the ground did not react to the magic. She lay in her bonds, the dark bruise on her forehead growing more pronounced by the minute.

Jey glanced over her shoulder as Elle straightened, swaying a little on her feet. Lokim had to resist the urge to go to her, to steady her. Jey fell back instead, offering her friend her arm. "We have to get back to the cheesery," she said. She stared off into the silver woods for a moment longer, then turned to Lokim. "You probably saved our lives tonight. How can we thank you?"

In the distance, an owl hooted. To the east, the rim of the sky was growing pale with the first tendrils of dawn. Lokim's eyes shifted from Jey to Elle. "Can we meet again?" he said. "To talk?"

As he spoke, a memory returned to him. It was of the very first night he saw Elle, almost a year ago now. He'd just arrived in Deramor. With Bliz stowed in his collar, he'd been prowling the streets, holding a passive echo spell to keep himself hidden. He'd walked into an alley outside a brightly lit mansion overflowing with guests. Elle had nearly startled him into a heart attack when she'd appeared before him, dropping her own passive echo spell and walking past him, unaware of his presence, to make her way out to join the party.

She hadn't been wearing her leathers that night. She'd been wearing a glittering gown. He'd tailed her, watching as she'd made her smooth way into the mansion. She'd spent hours in there. He'd waited in the shadows, watching for her. When she'd left, she'd done so by the more conventional means of stepping into a coach. Lokim had tailed the coach. It had led him back to the bridge across the river that led onto a walled island where hounds bayed in the night.

He looked at Elle and was struck silent with the force of all the questions he wanted to ask. He said, "I think we could help each other."

Nylan stared at the pale girl, trying to contain the hatred that seemed to boil inside him constantly now. The girl had a dark bruise on the left side of her temple. She could not tell him where it had come from.

The deployment node was dark except for one shuttered lantern. That had been part of the plan. Nylan knew the girls who had escaped were coming in. They had to be, because they would need the brillbane that was cultivated within the academy walls but had been eradicated beyond them as systematically and thoroughly as the tessili themselves.

For months, the academy had been flailing in ineffectual spasms. They'd increased patrols on the wall, set the hounds to sweeping the grounds day and night, and had orderlies watching the older girls 24/7. Such methods were not much, however, to defend against those who had already escaped, who could scale walls, make themselves invisible, and identify patterns of movement in order to work around them.

Part of the problem, Nylan suspected, was the orderlies and the administration, even the professors, didn't understand how dangerous and capable these girls were. Nylan knew. He, after all, had sent them out to accomplish impossible task after impossible task. And 99% of the time, they'd returned successful.

Which was why it was so frustrating, now, to have come so close only to be in danger of tripping at the finish line. Nylan had finally talked the dean into trying things his way, which was to make the academy inviting, to keep the hounds in their kennels, and to set other students—the most capable they had—to watch for their compatriots.

It had taken a month, but it had worked. This girl, M215, had caught the feeling of a spell being dropped at the base of the bridge. She remembered that much. She'd followed one of the escaped students, L134, and tracked her through the woods.

But then her memory cut off. She'd woken up back near the bridge with a headache and no recollection of anything else that had transpired.

Nylan had to resist the urge to hit the girl, to take her to the room where her tessila lay, weighted down by the heavy, padded harness that prevented it from dashing its ridiculous brains out, and forcing her to watch him break its tiny wings.

Realizing he was on the verge of losing his temper, Nylan turned his back on the girl. He limped away to look out one of the windows. The eastern sky was bright with dawn. His knee flared with pain as he moved. Even six months after the injury, the joint was not whole. The damage it had sustained from that one blow had been considerable. He was told he was lucky he was able to walk at all.

Nylan did not feel lucky. He felt precarious. Here he was, poised on the eve of the fruition of all his years of hard work and two teenaged girls were threatening to cost him everything.

That was the real problem here. Nylan's performance was under review. He was on probation, pending the recovery of the two lost operatives. An empty syringe had been found in the senior's dormitory, along with a stolen holdstone. One orderly knew Nylan himself had taken the syringe into the dormitory that night – the night he'd made the worst mistake of his life. And so far that orderly had not spoken.

If the man did speak, or if Nylan did not get the two missing operatives recaptured or neutralized, this would be Nylan's last year at the academy. Which would mean, if he was lucky, he would have wasted the last decade of his life. If he was unlucky it would mean the end of his life entirely.

Nylan stood for a while, listening to the quiet, scared breathing of the girl. With a frustrated growl, he turned to the desk and opened the top drawer. The glass bodies of syringes clinked as they rolled with the movement of the drawer. He pulled one out, closed the drawer, and approached the girl. "Roll up your sleeve," he said.

She did, though he could see the question in her eyes. He waited until her arm was turned towards him, the pale underside exposed. He plunged the syringe into a vein.

For one moment, Nylan hesitated. The drug was hard on the girls. It taxed both the heart and the nervous system. He'd seen some of them collapse into seizures over the years. A few had not gotten up again. This girl had already had one injection tonight. The possibility of an overdose was very real. Nylan couldn't afford to lose one of the two new seniors. Neither one of them showed much particular talent for anything, but they were all he had. And he still had work to do.

He didn't know if the drug would help. It stood to reason it might. The drug, after all, was a powerful psychosomatic stimulant, among other things. Unfortunately, Nylan was up against magic, not science. Magic was nothing if not unreasonable.

But Nylan also couldn't afford to lose the information this girl had, locked away somehow in her head.

The girl went rigid as Nylan depressed the stopper. She sucked in a quick breath and blinked several times.

Then she said in a quiet, dreamy voice, "I tracked her back to Deramor, to the outskirts, near the north road. Then someone hit me on the head. That's all I know."

Then, the girl collapsed.

◈

Jey scooped up a handful of cheese curds. A heap of molds lay on the long table before her, some full, some empty. She packed the curds into an empty mold, pressing them down evenly, as Holdam had taught her. Beside her, Elle was doing the same.

Phril was perched on Jey's shoulder. Although she couldn't see him, she could feel the small weight of him, the snag of his tiny talons in her homespun shirt. He was sulking again because she'd asked him not to fly. He could almost never fly these days. It was too risky. Passive echo spells did not work very well on tessili in general and became nearly useless when one was flying. Since it was critical Holdam and Biala never see Phril or Shai, the two tessili were commanded to lie low on a daily basis.

It was not a natural way for a tessila to live. Jey attributed that, and the lack of brillbane bushes, to Phril's recent bad temper. Though Jey and Elle managed to supply their tessili with the seeds they needed to survive, it was evident the small animals were suffering from not having access to brillbane bushes as a whole. Phril's scales were duller than Jey could remember ever seeing them, as he had no brillbane husk to polish himself against. He also didn't seem to sleep as well or as deeply now that he couldn't climb into the heart of one of the brushy plants and feel safe there.

These things were problems. They were problems on Jey's long, long list of problems. When they had escaped from the academy, it had been out of necessity. They'd been mere hours away from scheduled death. They run, not knowing what they were running into. Their situation was less dire now, but they were a long way from being able to feel safe.

"How is it he has a tessila but no one else we've seen since leaving the academy does?" Elle spoke in a voice barely above a whisper. She stood a few paces down from Jey, her dark hair tied back in a blue scarf.

Jey shrugged, setting the full mold aside and reaching for another. She felt dull with fatigue. Even when she and Elle had returned to their room and collapsed into their beds, she'd hardly slept. Discovery by the academy had always been a possibility, but knowing they'd come so close rattled her.

Jey had noticed, of course, when she'd been sent out on her opportunities to complete one mission or another, the people she encountered didn't have tessili. But it wasn't something she'd ever thought much about. She hadn't thought much about anything, in those days. She'd been unable to. The drugs and flashnodes in the academy had rendered her incapable of forming cohesive memories.

Now that they were outside the academy, Jey and Elle had discovered something they'd never suspected: tessili did not seem to exist out in the wider world. No one spoke of them. There was no brillbane, either in people's gardens or growing wild in the forest.

More than that, the very subject appeared to be taboo. Elle had discovered this the hard way when she'd asked Holdam what had seemed an innocent question about why there seemed to be so few tessili about. She'd dropped the inquiry into casual conversation on one of their first days at the cheesery. The man had turned white as whey, started shaking, and stammered that he and his wife had no love for magics and he didn't know why anyone would think he knew the first thing about tessili. He'd been so upset, Elle had cast a passive persuasion on him so he would forget the conversation.

That had been the real blow. Jey wanted nothing more than to leave, to head into the hills and see what lay beyond the next ridge. But she couldn't, because Phril needed brillbane to survive, and if Phril died, so would she.

The bare fact that another human being outside the academy had a bond with a tessila was a huge relief. The problem was, Jey didn't know if they could trust him.

"He must have access to brillbane," Elle continued. She was speaking in the tone she used when she was trying to wheedle Jey around to some conclusion she knew Jey would resist.

Jey thumped her full mold to settle the curds with a little more force than necessary. She felt Phril swell with the desire to flit about the room. She paused, closed her eyes for a moment, and took a deep breath. It made her tessila's difficult task harder when she let herself grow frustrated about their circumstances.

"He must," Jey agreed. Then she voiced the deep, secret fear that had been gnawing at her heart since the strange young man had materialized in their bedchamber. "But Elle, what if there's another academy? One for men? What if he's from there? What if he's a trap? What if the whole thing with catching the girl that followed you was staged, so we'd trust him? What if he's going to lead us straight into our enemies' hands?"

Elle froze in the act of pressing down some curd. The cheesery smelled of fresh milk and clover. It was a bright winter day, with brilliant sunlight falling in through the windows.

Elle looked pale and scared as she turned her large eyes to meet Jey's. She sounded tired and defeated when she said in a wan tone, "I never thought of that."

Jey frowned down at her cheese mold, feeling the scratchiness of her eyes. Phril had settled somewhat, but his desire to fly was a constant undercurrent in her thoughts – an itch she could not scratch.

They were silent for a moment. Outside, birds called in the clear sky. One of the dairy's goats bleated – a hungry sound. Elle dropped her voice to an even lower register and said, "How close are we, Jey? With what I collected last night?"

Jey shaped the soft, cool curds, calculating. "Close," she said. "We have enough seeds now. We need more cash."

There was a bang as the cheesery door swung open, making them both jump. Holdam shouldered his way into the room. The stocky, gray haired man stumped across the room carrying a bucket of fresh milk. He nodded a greeting at the girls, humming as he headed for the vats in the adjoining chamber. Jey nodded back, thoughts still on her conversation with Elle.

The frustrating thing was they were so close. They had a plan – a plan that should let them leave the academy behind for now, to live in peace. They needed to recover and grow and learn about this world they now had to live in.

But they weren't quite ready. As Holdam disappeared through the doorway she said to Elle, "The land grant hasn't been approved yet, either. We need our affirmation. "

Elle set a full mold aside, pausing to stretch her back. "More money should be easy enough to come by," she said. "And I'll persuade Holdam to draw up the document we need from him. Then we can go." She paused, meeting Jey's gaze and holding it for a beat.

Jey said, "And, if Lokim is not our friend, we'll need to find a way to get him off our tail."

Jey saw something flicker through Elle's eyes, a flutter of the deep fatigue Jey battled every day. They had been working towards their goal for months, making incremental progress each day. "Do you think they'll find us first?" Elle asked.

Jey turned to look out at the frozen yard. The fatigue seemed to grow for a moment, exerting a strange pressure on her heart. "I think it's only a matter of time. It's just a question of who is faster."

◈

They met Lokim again that night. They'd decided the safest place for a rendezvous was in their own chamber. It would be easy enough to hide Lokim if Biala came inquiring after their light, and Jey and Elle would have the advantage of being near all their weapons.

The girls retired early, earning a knowing smile from Biala when they begged fatigue as a reason to slip off to bed. They'd reached their chamber and settled down to wait, Jey perched on the wooden chair at the desk, Elle seated on the foot of her narrow bed. Phril and Shai, finally free of the directive not to fly, shot into the air and chased each other in circles around the small room.

As it was winter, the sun was already down. Elle and Jey waited in the light of their small flame. A litany of all the things she needed to guard against played on repeat in Jey's head. She was too tired, though, to be truly afraid. It was funny, she thought, how danger itself became less alarming after a while.

He didn't knock this time. The door opened and closed in one smooth movement. Jey, who had her knives set within easy reach on the table, sat up a little straighter.

He appeared within the door, as tall and straight as before. His tessila shot from his collar to join Phril and Shai in their happy flight. Jey could smell the man. He gave off a scent of wood smoke and earth. She resisted the urge to pick up her knives; she could tell he was going out of his way to appear non-threatening.

He nodded to the leaping flame in the dish of oil. "Perhaps it might be prudent to cast a passive barrier spell, to contain the light and the sound of our voices?"

Jey felt her discomfort increase. She glanced at the dish, as if considering his words. Elle, however, sat forward, leaning towards the man with a look of surprise. "Passive barrier?" Her long braid was a dark, smooth rope over one shoulder. "We never learned that one."

A flicker of surprise passed over Lokim's face, barely there before it was gone. Jey let out a silent sigh. In spite of their years in the academy, Elle was proving a little too quick to trust people.

Lokim said, "Allow me." He stood a little straighter. He did not otherwise move, but Jey felt the tug and dip of the spell as he wove and released. She had an instant to wonder if this would be the moment of betrayal. But it passed. The atmosphere in the room returned to normal, except Jey could feel a mild sheen of magic that remained in place around them like an invisible dome.

"Thank you," Elle said. Lokim settled down cross-legged on the floor. Broad back leaning against the stone wall, he broadcasted the air of someone who intended to stay. He had dark hair, a firm jaw and round, mild eyes. His face was nothing like the smooth-cheeked orderlies, the angry Nylan, or even the sophisticated, reserved Liam. This man was something else.

Jey's fatigue now warred with her curiosity, but she tried to keep her tone disinterested. "Where did you come from?" she said.

He didn't answer immediately. Phril, Shai, and the man's tessila were still darting about the room in some sort of complex pattern. Phril alighted on the windowsill. He sat for an instant, wings flared, neck arched, red scales gleaming in the wan light.

Lokim's eyes went to the tessila. "He's magnificent," he said. "I don't recognize his characteristics. What's his lineage?"

For the second time in only a few moments, Jey felt discomfited. Shai swooped towards Phril and the red tessila took to the air again. Jey watched the three diminutive animals dart about the room, feeling a tug-of-war taking place inside her. She wished she could trust this man without reservation, to accept the friendship he seemed to offer.

But she couldn't. She reminded herself what was at stake. If the academy had half a chance, they'd do to Jey and Elle what they'd done to Kae. That night still haunted Jey's nightmares – the night her friend had died.

Jey sat up a little straighter. "I'm afraid I don't know his lineage." She turned from the tessila back to Lokim. "We actually know next to nothing about our tessili. We were taken to the academy as girls, where tessili and brillbane are everywhere. It wasn't until we escaped we realized they are so rare out here."

Lokim's face darkened. His eyes were colorless in the darkness, his jaw shadowy with stubble. His hands, set on his knees, were rough and square. There was a ready tension in his body, and his muscles were firm from use. "They didn't used to be rare." The words came out in a low tone, heavy with sadness.

Elle sat forward further so she was perched on the edge of the bed. "What happened?"

The young man looked up. His eyes met Elle's and held for what seemed to Jey a long time. "The Betrayal," he said at last. "The people of Masidon turned against the Tessilari after we all stood together through the War of the Diods. Our numbers were reduced with the fighting, our strongest mages weakened or killed. We gave our best and our strongest to keep this land safe. Then the people turned against us. Tessili were hunted, brillbane was uprooted and burned. Tessilari were hunted down and murdered."

Elle's eyes had widened at Lokim's words. "Why?" she said. "Why would they attack their allies after a war was won?"

Lokim's firm mouth turned down at the edges. He dropped his gaze to the floor. "Fear," he said. "When the diods appeared, the people of Masidon welcomed them. But the diods were brutal, their magics violent and destructive. It nearly destroyed the Tessilari to destroy them. After that, some people became convinced all magic was evil. Most particularly, the church. The high priest declared humans who could wield magics were an affront to the gods."

Jey shifted in her seat, thinking of the hours she and Elle had wasted hunting for brillbane that wasn't there. She repeated her initial question. "Then where do you come from?"

Lokim turned his sharp gaze on her. "The vast majority of our people died in the Betrayal, but a small band of refugees escaped. We've lived apart ever since, confined to one hidden valley. We thought we were the last of the Tessilari, that the tessili we saved were the only ones."

As he spoke, Phril came to perch on Jey's shoulder. She could feel his excitement, his pleasure with the flight, his curiosity about the orange tessila who had a bond with Lokim.

Lokim watched Phril for a moment, then glanced around the room as if looking for something. "How are you keeping them fed?" But before either of them could answer, his eyes widened with understanding. "That's why you keep going back over the wall."

Jey lifted one hand to Phril. He stepped onto her fingers. She held him before her so she could run one finger under his chin, noting his dull scales and thin sides. "It's the only place we know to get brillbane."

Lokim sat very still for a moment. His face was immobile, his eyes flat, but Jey perceived he was coming to a decision.

At last, he closed his eyes. He held them closed for what seemed a long time. "I jeopardize my people by showing this to you," he said. Then he let out a small, sad laugh. "But then, I jeopardized my people when I left the valley."

He moved, reaching inside the neck of his shirt. A silver chain glittered in the yellow light. He drew out a thin wire ring and held it up in the air before him. His tessila, with a glad little cry, turned on the air. With a dip of her wings, she banked, beat twice, and shot straight through the ring.

She did not come out the other side.

Jey blinked, staring at the plain ring. Her feeling was one of mild puzzlement until Phril, with a sudden surge of excitement so intense it was a sharp pain in Jey's mind, leapt off her hand and beat towards the ring as well.

Jey felt her heart go still. The moment seemed to extend as if time had slowed. Jey reached after the tessila, as if she could snatch him from the air.

Lokim saw the tessila coming, but he did not lower the ring. He continued to hold it up.

Phil darted through its center and disappeared.

CHAPTER 3

Lokim hadn't planned for it to happen. He hadn't planned on revealing any secrets tonight. Even before Jey asked about how he fed his tessila and kept her happy, he'd said too much. Now he'd gone ahead and shown them his stitchring, and Jey's tessila had followed Bliz through.

Elle was the problem. After so many months watching her from a distance, being near her was like a drug. Every time he looked over and saw her looking at him with those bright eyes, his brain seemed to fizz. He would lose track of his train of thought, or say something he'd meant to hold back. It was even more intoxicating that Elle seemed to trust him already, in a way Jey did not. He could see the little flickers of displeasure in Jey's face every time Elle said something that revealed more of their situation.

Now, unsurprisingly, Elle's tessila wheeled on the air, realizing he'd been left alone. It was clear from the girls' faces they didn't know what a stitchring was. Jey had gone pale and had risen out of her chair, hands moving to take up her knives. "Lower the ring," she said.

Lokim looked at Elle. He knew her tessila was purple, but the dim light leeched the color from the room.

He didn't lower the ring.

Elle's tessila turned and poured on speed, black eyes intense. Jey moved forward, her stance threatening, but Lokim was not afraid.

It took a fraction of an instant for Elle's tessila to dart across the room and dive through the ring, following the other two. Lokim felt the drag on his reserves as the spell activated for the third time in quick succession. Fatigue seemed to crush him. The stitchring cost him a good deal.

His vision went a little dark around the edges. He was aware both Jey and Elle were now staring at him in mute horror. He was aware he needed to explain, to reassure them. He should have done that first.

But for a moment, he was too tired to speak. Then he felt Bliz's delight at not only settling onto her brillbane bush, but having company. In spite of the fact they were now very far apart, geographically, the stitchring allowed him to feel as if she was only on the other side of the room.

Lokim lowered the ring so it hung outside his shirt, glinting in the dancing light. Both the girls had been made into statues by the shock. He said, "I'm sorry. I didn't think. Elle, if I'd tried to keep your tessila from following the others he'd have gone frantic with frustration."

Elle's fine chin dipped in the barest hint of a nod. But she was never the one he was going to have trouble convincing. He closed his eyes for a moment, preparing to face Jey. In truth, this was the greatest help he could offer them at the moment. Their tessili were alive, but the more he'd seen of them the more he'd noticed the brittle edge to their movements, the frantic tension in their eyes. If the girls only stole brillbane seeds from behind the wall, it must have been six months since either of their tessila had had a proper rest.

"It's a stitchring," he said. "It connects two places. This one allows Bliz to visit her brillbane bush in a greenhouse in the valley where my people live. She can feed and rest and polish her scales."

Elle's face creased with concern. She'd evidently noticed the strain on his face. He avoided looking at her, but the desire to do so was there, an electric undercurrent beneath his fatigue.

He looked at Jey. She'd set her knives back down and was staring at the ring with an intense expression.

She had to be getting feedback from her tessila by now. She had to know he was unharmed. The tessila himself would present a more persuasive argument than Lokim could.

Lokim stretched his back and settled more comfortably against the wall. He said, "They'll come back when they're ready. In the meantime, we may as well talk."

◈

As much as Jey might try to deny it, the change in
Phril when he emerged from the thing Lokim called a
stitchring the next morning was undeniable.

The humans had called it a night long before.
Lokim had made his bed on the floor using Jey's cloak as
a cushion, Elle's as a pillow, and his own as a blanket. Jey
and Elle had gone to their beds. Jey had blown out the
flame and the three of them had occupied the silent
darkness. Jey had been unable to relax for fear of Lokim
leaving and taking the stitchring with him.

Before they'd gone to sleep, they'd talked. They'd
talked and talked. During their conversation, Jey had
slowly lost the battle of keeping secrets, of holding back,
of being selective about how they revealed their
weaknesses. The problem, she reflected, was how badly
she wanted an ally. To simply be able to talk to someone
about the predicament she and Elle found themselves in
was a scale of relief so profound it made her giddy.

In the end, Jey lay in the dark with her head
spinning, then dozed off without meaning to. When she
woke, the pale light of dawn was spilling in through the
window. Lokim was asleep, a dark form under his cloak.
Elle was also asleep, curled under her gray blanket.

The tessili hadn't reappeared. They didn't do so until the last minute, when Jey was starting to feel frantic about the need to go to the cheesery and start their day's work. She and Elle, having never undressed the night before due to Lokim's presence, had tidied themselves as best they could. Although Lokim had discreetly not watched, Jey had felt self-conscious, nonetheless, as she'd brushed out her hair and tied it back in its ponytail.

When Phril, Shai, and Bliz had returned at last, they'd done so in a brilliant cluster, bursting out of the ring to soar about the room. Phril was transformed. His scales were bright, his sides were not as hollow as they had been. More importantly, that frantic edge was gone from his mind. His thoughts were settled and mellow, like they'd used to be.

Jey hadn't realized how much Phril's distress had been affecting her. Now, as he came to her, she could feel his satisfaction as she noted the brightness of his red hide. He landed on her outstretched hand and strutted a little. It broke her heart that he'd been brought so low.

Lokim rose, smiling as his slim orange tessila, Bliz, flew to him. Shai looked rested and content as well. For a moment, Jey felt almost happy.

Then they heard the sound of Holdam breaking the ice on the water trough across the yard. Jey felt her smile fade.

Lokim was looking at Elle as he tucked the ring back inside his shirt. "When can I see you again?" He spoke in a whisper, with an intensity that made the dormant unease stir in Jey's heart.

Elle was blushing, her eyes downcast. She did not consult Jey before saying, "Will you come back tonight?"

Lokim's answer was a quick nod. Then he cast a passive echo spell. His body shimmered on the air, disappearing. Bliz took a moment longer to fade as she wheeled up to land and tuck her brilliant body beneath his collar.

A moment later, the door opened, then closed.

He was gone.

Elle let out a sigh and sank down to sit on her bed again. Her dress, usually tidy, had a rumpled look. Jey looked at her friend in consternation. "Tonight?" she said. Her eyes were scratchy with fatigue. "When are we going to sleep?"

Elle was still looking at the floor. She shrugged, as if her thoughts were far away. Shai was preening himself on her shoulder, radiating well-rested satisfaction. "It's the best thing for Phril and Shai." She spoke in a quiet tone, but her cheeks were still flushed red.

Jey looked at her friend, the uneasy feeling growing. It occurred to her for the first time that she and Elle were together now because they always had been. Almost all of

Jey's memories, patchy as they were, included Elle and Kae. The three girls had come to the academy the same year, learned at the same rate. They'd slept in the same room, attended many of the same classes, and spent all their leisure time together. They'd had no choice.

Out here, though, beyond the academy walls, they did have a choice. Jey and Elle could come to different decisions about things. They could even part ways.

The thought sent a shiver of fear snaking up Jey's spine. She didn't argue Elle's point, but she couldn't help making one comment as she stooped to tie on her boots. "We won't be truly free, Elle, until we rely on no one. Not even Lokim."

The words hung in the dawning room. Elle said nothing. A few minutes later, they left to start their day.

Elle moved down the busy street, marveling at the easy flow of the crowd. There were so many people in Deramor. All her life, Elle had lived in quiet seclusion. The academy had been vast and mostly empty. Now, life at the cheesery was removed from the thrum and bustle of Masidon's capital. That was one of the reasons she and Jey had chosen it as a place to go to ground.

One good thing, Elle reflected as she stepped around a woman who had stopped to collar a straying child, was the fact that the other student who tracked them back to this city could hardly give the academy much more of a lead in finding them. Deramor was the only city of any size in the entire country (she had learned this fact from Lokim the night before). The expanse of Masidon's land, between the two seas to the north and south, the mountains to the west, and the sands to the east, had been all but depopulated by the Two Wars.

Thinking of all they'd learned from Lokim the previous night, Elle felt a tremor of unease. At the same time she felt a little thrill shoot through her, as so often happened when she thought of Lokim. She pulled her hood forward a little further, glad the biting wind gave her an excuse to hide her face.

Shai was tucked inside her wide sleeve, clinging to the inside of the fabric and watching the street with keen eyes. For the first time in weeks, he felt content to hold still.

Elle reached a crossroads and turned right, winding her way further into the heart of the city. As she continued, the streets grew broader, the buildings larger, more ornate, and statelier. At last she stopped before a wide building with the words, "LANDS & ESTATES" etched into the stone above the door. Next to the door hung a painted sign – the same one that had caught her eye months ago:

> **Land Grant Opportunity**
> Any citizen possessing the necessary capital and avowed by a tradesman of having mastered a food-producing skill may apply for leave to occupy an abandoned estate. Inquire for details within.

Elle's heart gave another lurch as she read the sign again. She let out a quick breath and pushed through the large wooden doors.

The space behind the door was dim and vast. Citizens stood in a line, waiting for the attention of one of three clerks who sat behind the wooden counter. It was quiet in the room. The citizens who waited did so in silence.

Elle looked around, searching for the clerk she'd spoken to the last time she'd been in. She felt a surge of relief when she recognized him. She got in line and waited, keeping at least part of her attention on Shai the whole time to help ensure he didn't do anything rash.

The line was slow and the wait dragged. Around her, people coughed and shuffled their feet, and Elle's mind strayed again to Lokim.

He was such a mystery. Even after what he'd told them the night before, about coming from a hidden valley, Elle couldn't wrap her mind around what his life must be like. Did he have friends back in the valley? Parents? Siblings? A girlfriend? He had such nice eyes. They were deep and dusky, kind of like his voice. She wondered how old he was.

"Next, please."

The clerk who had spoken was not the one Elle wanted to talk to, but Elle looked up with surprise to find herself at the font of the line. Flustered, she pretended to consult the documents in the leather case she carried. She turned to look at the man behind her. "Go ahead." she suggested. He gave her a puzzled look but moved around her to the impatient clerk.

Elle, cheeks blazing, found herself standing with a pounding heart. She looked around the room for something to keep her thoughts more focused, but there was little enough to look at. The shield and crest of Masidon hung on the wall above the clerks. The wall by the door contained posters and signs of various shapes and sizes, none of which were close enough for Elle to read.

At last, a woman walked away from the counter. The young clerk Elle had been waiting for looked up with an expression of expectation. She lifted her chin and stepped forward.

The clerk was a slim man with delicate hands, pale skin, and light hair. His body had none of the firm look of use that Lokim's had. He looked at her without much interest as she moved forward and leaned against the counter. "How can I help you today, miss?" His tone was pleasant, if bored.

Elle opened her folder and drew out the missive she'd come to deliver. She handed it across to him. "My cousin and I applied for a land grant a few months ago. This is our endorsement from a tradesman." She struggled not to blush as she said the words. As much as Holdam liked her and Jey, there was no chance he ever would have endorsed them as cheese-making professionals. She'd magicked him into doing it – a fact for which she felt guilty.

The clerk took the document, glanced at it, and set it on a pile to one side. "Thank you," he said, tone brisk now, as if to imply all was done. "You'll receive a summons when it's time for you to deliver your capital and receive the grant."

It was clear he expected her to step aside. Elle, faint with anxiety, reached out and set one finger on his delicate wrist. The young man froze, looking at her. Elle wove a small spell – a small thing to make him more tractable. "Please, I was wondering," she said, trying to keep her voice light and innocent, "if there was any way we could hurry the process along. My cousin and I are anxious, you see, to start our new life."

The man looked at her. He squinted as if having trouble focusing his eyes. He blinked once, slowly, and looked again at her finger on his wrist. She wove another little passive persuasion, releasing it into him gently.

He sat up a little straighter. "Yes, of course," he said. Then he leaned forward and said in a confidential tone, "Some of these sit here for weeks before anyone looks at them. Bureaucracy, you know. Delari knows, it's slow because everyone's lazy. I'll see yours goes straight to the top of the pile."

He winked. Elle managed a queasy smile. She withdrew her hand, thanking him and moving off so the next citizen could approach the desk.

As she headed towards the door, she pulled her hood back up, letting her eyes wander over the array of people who waited in line. All of them had dreams, she supposed. Some of them might be in situations as urgent as her own. And she'd cheated her way in front of everyone else.

With a small sigh, Elle slipped out the door, moved down the shallow stone steps, and blended back into the jumble of bodies outside.

She didn't notice the slender girl who stood in the shadow of a doorway across the street, hooded and cloaked, and watching her.

The black goat butted Jey in the chest with its flat forehead. Jey grunted. It was a friendly gesture, she knew by now. But still. The goat had a remarkably solid skull.

Jey sidled around the cluster of goats, bearing her pitchfork. They lost interest in her as she began to sift through the scattered straw inside their enclosure. She picked out damp spots and spread bedding that had collected into drifts. When she ran out of that occupation, she wandered over to the skewbald half draft horse who stood dozing in the corner. Holdam kept him for pulling the cart. He was a docile giant with feathered feet and a kind eye. She gave him a pat on the neck, then moved behind him to finger-comb his tail.

Throughout her time in the pen, Jey jumped at every sound. She glanced frequently towards the gate in the wall of the side yard, waiting for it open, letting her know Elle had returned unscathed. She did not like it when Elle ventured into the city alone. Elle's aptitudes were more subtle than Jey's. She was accomplished at the sorts of interpersonal manipulations Jey tended to blunder, but she wasn't nearly as effective when diplomacy failed and it came time for violence.

Jey left the horse, retrieved her pitchfork, and reversed it in her hands. She used the end of the handle the chip away at the remains of the ice in the water trough. She was stalling. The pen had a good vantage of the gate. Jey wanted to watch the gate until Elle returned, in case she was followed.

They took precautions against this, of course. They never walked openly back to the cheesery after spending time in town. They always headed first in some random direction, ducked into an alleyway, cast a passive echo spell, and retraced their steps.

But passive echo spells were not foolproof. Jey herself could see through them sometimes, if the conditions were right.

The red goat wandered over to sniff at the hem of her skirt. Phril bristled. He was tucked into a crease at her waistline. He hissed at the offending animal for coming too near.

The goat paid the tessila no heed. Jey lifted a foot to nudge the animal away. She'd learned early these creatures could do a terrific amount of damage to a set of skirts in a small amount of time if she let their inquisitive nibbling go unchecked.

As Jey was looking down at the goat, she heard the telltale click of the gate's latch. She turned, heart going still, and saw nothing. The gate swung open enough for a slim person to pass through. It closed again just as quickly.

Jey, relieved, made her exit from the pen. She tossed the soiled straw into the compost heap, hung the pitchfork on its hook, and hurried across the yard. She could hear Holdam whistling as he worked the churn. She knew Biala was in town, making deliveries. Elle had been making deliveries as well, fitting the extra errand around her other duties.

Jey went to the gate, intending to peek out into the quiet lane to ensure no one was out there. She approached the wall, glanced behind her to make sure Holdam was out of sight, and reached for the latch.

The gate hit her as she extended her hand. She jumped back with a quick curse. Heart pounding with sudden terror, she reached for the small knife she kept tucked in her bodice. It was a tiny thing, by necessity. But Jey could inflict a lot of damage with a small, sharp blade.

The gate clicked closed. No person was visible. Jey narrowed her eyes, watching for signs of someone cloaked in a passive echo spell. Her knife was in her hand, her every sense strained for evidence of the intruder.

The ground was damp. As she watched, she saw the soft earth depress under the weight of a boot.

"Jey, it's me." Lokim's voice was a hard whisper near her ear. It startled her so badly she almost lashed out with the knife. Phril, goaded by her agitation, hissed again, barely containing his desire to fly out of his hiding place and attack.

Jey contained herself with some effort. Her heart was pounding. Phril's desire to fight was a heat behind her eyes. Her voice grated out in a harsh whisper. "I thought you weren't coming back until tonight."

She was still watching the ground. The depression where she thought Lokim's boot was eased a little, another appearing nearby. His voice was slightly further away when he replied. "I followed Elle. And someone followed her."

Jey moved along the wall, ducking behind the pump house, trusting Lokim to follow her. She heard the swish of his trouser legs and saw some dry grasses bend as he passed near them.

When they'd made it around the corner of the pump house, they were concealed between the cheesery wall and the corner of the building. Jey said, "Who followed her? Did they track her back here?"

It was annoying, Jey decided, to talk to someone who was invisible. In spite of knowing where he was, Jey couldn't penetrate Lokim's spell. His words drifted back to her, low and unhappy.

"It was another girl. Not the same one as before. She was watching the Lands & Estates office. Elle lost her when she went into a sweets shop, out into the alley, and cast her passive echo spell. The girl waited outside the shop for a while, checked inside, then headed out of town. I came back here. Is Elle here? Is she safe?"

Elle appeared, then, as if summoned by her name. She came strolling out from the main residence where Biala and Holdam lived, carrying a broom, her hair pulled back in a scarf.

Jey chewed her lip, not sure whether to be annoyed at Lokim for continuing to dog their heels or grateful for the intelligence. She didn't have time to decide. Hearing Elle, Holdam poked his head out the cheesery doors. "Girls," he called in his friendly voice. "Time to pack some curds."

Jey shot a look in Lokim's general direction. "You stay out of sight," she warned him, as if he wasn't doing that already. Then she sighed, turned, and stepped out from behind the pump house.

CHAPTER 4

"They were watching the land office." Lokim said the words with a kind of desperation. He'd said them several times already as he paced around their small chamber, filling it with his restlessness and that smell of wood and smoke and earth.

Jey was in the chair, Elle sitting on her bed. The three tessili had darted through the stitchring the moment Lokim had pulled it from his shirt. Jey found it a little hurtful that Phril thought so little of leaving her. But she pushed the feeling aside. She had more important things to worry about.

"Yes, Lokim." Jey was having trouble containing her annoyance. He'd been at them since the moment they returned to their chamber, arguing, prodding, trying to get them to leave. He felt they were no longer safe at the cheesery, that it was only a matter of time before the academy's forces descended on them. "But they didn't track us here."

Elle was the most subdued presence in the room. She sat on her bed, the soft wave of her hair falling to conceal most of her face. She seemed to feel it was her fault they were in jeopardy.

Lokim's voice had gained a desperate edge. "I have been in Deramor for a year now. Before I found you, I spent my time learning the politics of this place. Some of the Tessilari believe it's time we came out of hiding. I left my people to learn who we might need to influence to change the laws that condemn all who practice magic. I have spent months coming to understand the different sects in the government, the groups who oppose one another in public, and those who collaborate behind closed doors. Do you know what I have found? Your academy doesn't exist. The government does not oversee what happens there. But the church does know, and it is using the academy to its own ends."

The young man paused, glancing from Elle to Jey and back again. When neither one spoke or betrayed any surprise at his statement, he continued in a rush. "Did you never wonder, Jey, how I knew to wait for you in that lord's chamber the night I hurt your arm? I was waiting there because all the members of the House of Laws had been slowly changing their minds, one by one, about an issue all of them should have adamantly opposed on principle. I put two and two together and began to shadow that man, thinking I'd uncover who was bribing or threatening his peers. Instead, you appeared, and I finally understood. That is what you were there for that night, wasn't it? To change the way that man cast his vote?"

Jey hesitated, feeling unmoored all of a sudden. The information Lokim had just dumped on her felt too large, too overwhelming to process. She only said, "Yes."

Lokim went on. "The church uses the academy to push its agenda, and so it has become tremendously powerful. You've left a paper trail, leading straight back here, and they now know where it starts. They will be here any minute now. We should have left already."

Jey closed her eyes. She was so tired. She was tired in so many ways. She hadn't had enough sleep in days. It seemed she was always having to make choices, to weigh options, to decide on the safest path forward. And the stakes were too high. One mistake could mean death.

"The clerk said he'd hurry things along." Elle's words were soft, the first contribution she'd made to the discussion in some time. "It should be soon, Jey. We should be able to go soon."

Jey looked at her friend for a moment, noting the droop in her shoulders, the blank look in her usually bright eyes. She was tired too.

Lokim turned to glare at Jey. For some reason, he was directing the full force of his arguments at her. "Not quickly enough. Don't you see? They will be here tonight. What do you think will happen if they find you here? You might escape, but what about these people who have taken you in? Would you bring death down on their heads?"

Jey stirred, her conscience pricked. Elle looked up as well, voicing the reality Jey hadn't spoken. "Lokim," Elle said. "We have nowhere else to go."

The comment hung in the dim room. It seemed too still and somber within those stone walls without the tessili dancing on the air to liven things up.

Lokim let out a frustrated breath. "I've been telling you, I can take you to my people."

Jey shook her head. During their longer conversation the night before, Lokim had told them much. He'd explained about the War of the Diods, the Betrayal, and the systematic extermination of the tessili. He'd explained about how the realm had descended into near chaos for a time and how the three house system of government now worked.

What he'd said very little about was himself and the hidden valley of the Tessilari. The things he had said (hidden, secret) sounded too much like the academy for Jey's taste. It sounded like relinquishing the freedom she'd fought so hard to gain. She would not go there, she'd already decided. Not if she could help it.

"No," Jey said, interceding before Elle could say anything. She looked up at Lokim. For a moment she tried to let all the fatigue, all the fear, all the uncertainty she was feeling show in her face. "I don't trust you yet, Lokim. I'm sorry."

A look of annoyed indignation came onto Lokim's face, but it faded. His dark eyes seemed to soften. He let out a long, weary sigh. He spoke in a voice that was low but earnest. "I sometimes forget what you've been through."

The flame on the desk danced. Outside, the night was still and cold. It would have been a good night for the kind of opportunity Jey used to be sent on for the academy. No one stirred out of doors in this kind of weather unless absolutely necessary.

The stillness made Jey uneasy. She couldn't deny that Lokim was right. It was only a matter of time before they were discovered.

As if reading her thoughts, Lokim spoke again. "At least come to my hideout, for now. Leave this place. We can work the rest out later."

The cheesery was quiet and dark. It was a wild night, with a cold wind gusting down the frozen streets and a bright, pale moon high in the sky. Lokim and Jey stood side by side in the front hall of Holdam and Biala's house, waiting. Elle had slipped into the couple's bedroom. She was even now weaving the spells that would make them forget they had ever known two girls hoping to learn the art of cheese making.

It was the only way to have any hope of keeping them safe. Jey saw that as clearly as she saw the silver slab of the wall across the courtyard. Still, she couldn't help but feel a pang at what they were losing. In some ways, Holdam and Biala were the first friends she'd ever had.

She sighed and tried to turn her thoughts. Lokim was a dark shape next to her. He was positioned in front of a window, staring out into the night. He was carrying a bulky bundle – a portion of the belongings Jey and Elle had divvied up to carry. There was an earnest set to his shoulders that was undeniably endearing.

Jey shook her head at the direction her thoughts had taken. She realized with a strange sense of surprise that she was starting to like Lokim. Worse, she and Elle seemed to rely on him more with each passing day. That was all right, she supposed, if he proved to be what he said he was. But if he wasn't?

Behind them, the bedroom door creaked as it opened. Elle ghosted into the hall on silent feet. In her eyes, there was something of the sadness Jey herself had been feeling. She spoke in a dull, tired tone. "They won't remember, now."

Jey looked into her friend's face with some concern. It would have been a lot of spellwork. And indeed, Elle's face was pale, her eyes a little vague. "Are you all right, Elle?"

Next to her, Lokim went stiff. "Passive echo spells. Now," he hissed. He moved closer to both of them, backing them into a dim corner where coats hung on pegs. Jey didn't waste time trying to see what had spooked him. She threw up her spell, extending it to cover the depleted Elle as well. Then she felt a strange, shimmery shock as her magic bumped and rubbed against Lokim's. He was shielding Elle too.

There was no time to comment on it. They were no sooner settled in their dark corner when the latch on the door clicked. It was locked, however, and the lock held.

Jey herself wore one of the backpacks she and Elle had stolen from the academy so long ago. They hadn't dared leave any trace of themselves in the room. She shifted the straps on her shoulders, feeling tense and claustrophobic in the crowded corner. She could feel her pack pressing into Elle's side. Lokim's shoulder was mere inches away from her mouth. She whispered, "How long can you hold a passive echo?"

There was a pause and a series of clicks. Jey recognized the sound of someone using a set of picks.

The shoulder moved up and down in a small shrug. "Twenty, thirty minutes, if I'm fresh."

Jey blinked, glad the darkness would conceal her surprise. She herself had rarely been able to hold a passive echo spell for more than five minutes. Elle's stamina was even less.

There wasn't time to discuss the point. There was a sharp click as the lock on the door gave way. The door cracked open.

One of the academy students slipped into Holdam and Biala's entry hall, wearing the telltale dark cloak and the smooth leathers. The girl was slender, but Jey knew underneath that cloak was a lean body, firm with muscle. She could well remember the hours and hours of training, with weapons and without, that had made her own body tough and lithe.

The girl stood inside the door for a moment, her face a shadowy outline in the moonlit entryway. Her head turned as she took in the hallway, the arched entrance to the kitchen, and the dark, empty corner in front of the coat hooks.

Jey could feel the pounding of her heart in her ears. Although she knew she was invisible, she'd never felt so exposed in her life.

The girl's attention drifted towards them, then past. She stalked into the kitchen.

A soft nudge in the small of her back told Jey they were moving. She wanted to protest. It seemed premature, but she heard the swish of Elle's skirts as her friend went with Lokim. Biting back a curse, she followed.

Lokim must have done something to the latch. It didn't click as it opened. He held the door for them and snugged it shut once she and Elle were outside.

In the cheesery yard, the wind hit Jey's face like a knife. Frost glittered along the paving stones and the top of the wall. The gusts filled her ears with white noise. She had a sudden moment of vertigo. She stared around the dark yard in disorientation, uncertain if the others were moving ahead or not.

Then she felt Lokim's warm, rough hand bumping into her arm. With a feeling of mixed impatience and relief, she let him find and grasp her hand. Together, the three of them walked across the yard.

At the front, the entrance to the cheesery was an open arch. There were gates, but Jey had never seen them shut. The arch was wide enough the three of them could pass through without letting go of each other.

They stepped through the arch and into the frozen streets of Deramor.

Jey felt some of the pressure of fear leave her shoulders. She glanced to the left and saw nothing but the sheen of moonlight glinting on cobblestones.

She glanced to the right and saw the hounds.

◈

Lokim felt a drag on his hand as Jey stiffened. It was remarkable, the difference in the two girls' grips. Elle's hand was soft. Though he could feel the strength in her fingers and he knew, from having watched her, how agile and tough she was, something about her touch felt timid.

Jey's hand, however, had an energy to it – a feeling of restless tension that seemed to communicate up his whole arm. When her steps lagged, her grip tightened on his.

There was a strange yip on the night air. It was a sound Lokim had heard before.

He had been looking up the street, scanning the road, the rooftops, and the shadows for any sign of life. As he turned his head, he saw movement over his shoulder.

And he saw the dogs.

There were at least five of them, tall creatures with tapered muzzles and fierce eyes. They stood on slender legs, heads raised as they stared around the dark street. There were two men with them, dressed in strange robes that flapped about their ankles in the wind.

"Those are sighthounds." Jey's whisper was difficult to catch in the restless air. "They can't follow unless they see us. But the scenthounds won't be far behind."

Lokim didn't waste more time. He tugged the girls forward.

The cheesery was at the outer edge of Deramor. The streets were not as dense with buildings here as they were within the city wall. Tradesmen lived on these lanes, their houses surrounded by grounds and yards, some walled or fenced, some not.

An orchard stood across from the cheesery. The family that lived there produced preserves and fresh fruit. Their lands were fenced, but the fence was low.

It was the only way forward, in any case. The cheesery wall stood at their backs. Going deeper into the city would give them fewer options. The pack of dogs blocked their way out of town.

They reached the fence. Lokim felt strangely unmoored when, one after the other, Jey and Elle took their hands from his. He heard the swish of fabric, a thump of a boot on the ground. He set his own hands on the wood. It was weathered and cracked, rough beneath his palms. He stepped up onto the bottom rail and swung his body over. Then he walked into the swaying shadows at the base of the fruit trees.

He paused to look back towards the cheesery. The men and their tall dogs had not come any closer. The girl was still searching within. They had a small window of time.

Lokim turned to see Elle standing, completely visible, only a few yards away. Her face was pale in the moonlight. She had the dazed look of someone who has lost her grip on a spell. He hurried to her and put his arm around her shoulders, letting his own passive echo spell conceal her again. Jey's voice spoke out of the darkness nearby. "She's over extended."

Elle's shoulders felt narrow within the wrap of Lokim's arm. The tossing wind brought him the scent of her hair, then snatched it away. For one long, sad moment, Lokim was filled with a longing for a different reality: one where their lives weren't in danger and he and Elle could find somewhere warm and quiet and spend the night talking about all the unimportant things they did not yet know about each other.

"We need to get to my hideout. Here." Lokim extended his hand, reaching out into the night and pulling his passive echo spell back a little so it could be seen. The instant he felt Jey's hand set into his, he started forward.

Although Elle didn't speak, she moved with him readily enough. They headed deeper into the orchard, moving along a row of trunks. The branches overhead were bare, black fingers between them and the silver sky.

But Jey's hand was still dragging on his. Lokim wasn't moving quickly, guiding and supporting Elle as he was, but Jey seemed always one step behind.

They left the first grove of trees and entered another – this one of scrubbier, lower shrubs with bristling branches. Once they crossed into the new rows, Jey gave a gasp and let her passive echo spell drop. She pulled her hand out of Lokim's and turned to look back.

Lokim paused, looking towards the cheesery. He could see nothing but swaying shadows and the high, cold moon. He said, "Jey, we need to hurry."

But Jey was shaking her head. Her light hair was shorter than Elle's and she wore it in a ponytail instead of a braid. The wind whipped it back and forth over her shoulder now, like a playful cat batting at a string. "You don't understand," Jey said. "They brought the hounds."

As if to emphasize her words, a single, silver-toned bay filled the night air. It was a clear noise. It rang over the blast of the wind – filled with a haunting sense of desire.

Lokim was barely containing the urge to grab Jey's hand and yank her around, to force her to continue forward. "Exactly," he hissed. "We need to get out of here."

Jey turned to look at him. There was something sad and hollow in her face. When she spoke, her words seemed to settle like cold rocks in stomach. "Hurrying won't make any difference now. With a trail this fresh, we'll never be able to throw them off our scent."

Lokim frowned. Elle made a small whimper and turned her head inward, as if to hide it against Lokim's shoulder. Lokim felt he was missing something.

"How did you do it before?" He said. "You escaped from the academy, right? They must have sent the hounds after you then."

Jey turned back to stare through the dark orchard. "They did," she said. "We killed them."

◈

Jey turned to walk through the wild night. She did not hurry.

"But I've seen you," Lokim said. "We can use the stream, go through the water."

Jey was still shaking her head. "That's just a precaution. If they don't find the trail for a few days, if the conditions are right, such tricks can throw them off. But this …" she gestured back over her shoulder towards the road. "They're right behind us. That kind of thing will never work."

There was a silence. Their footsteps were bare thumps on the frozen ground, the wind a constant presence. Those things would help slow down the inevitable, but they wouldn't be enough. "What we need to do," Jey said, "is find a defensible position."

Lokim stopped walking to stare at her, Elle still encircled by his arm. "What do you mean?"

Another bell-toned bay rose up towards the moon. If their trackers had found the room where Elle and Jey had lived for the last many months, there would be no difficulty getting the dogs onto the right scent.

Which meant they didn't have much time. "The only way to get these hounds off our trail," Jey said, "is to kill them." She tried to keep her voice firm and steady as she said the words, but inside, she felt a tremor of distaste. Memories returned to her – those first terrified nights she and Elle had spent running and hiding. They'd tried everything they could to shake the hounds.

Nothing had worked. In the end, they'd found themselves fighting for their lives more than once. At first, the dogs and handlers had been incautious, blundering upon the girls unprepared. After losing a few valuable scent dogs, however, the tactics shifted. Now the handlers were slower – taking their time, watching for ambushes, sending a student or two to range ahead so the defenseless dogs weren't in the most vulnerable position.

In spite of the fact Jey had been trained as an assassin, she did not like killing. She didn't like killing the men who hunted her, but she liked destroying the blameless dogs even less.

Still, the animals were relentless. Once on a scent, they were unshakeable. And if the orderlies got close enough to release their sighthounds ….

Jey shuddered, fingers straying over her left forearm where an array of silver scars decorated the skin. She'd been torn up one night trying to evade a dog without hurting it. She wouldn't make that mistake again.

Lokim was still looking at Jey, frowning. "Don't they sniff along the ground?" he said. "I mean, if we could get off the ground, would we be safe?"

They were still walking, passing tree after three. The orchard would be a terrible place to fight. Dogs could come at them from all directions, surround them and hold them there until the orderlies with stunrods could come upon them. She answered Lokim absently. "They sniff the ground, yes, but they also sniff the air. They can follow a scent on the wind. Believe me, Lokim, we tried everything. They can't be tricked."

Ahead of them, the scrubby trees ended and transitioned into a grove full of slender silver trunks. Behind them, all had gone quiet. Which meant the hounds were coming, eating up the ground at their steady shuffle.

Still under Lokim's protective arm, Elle stumbled. Lokim spoke, his voice a little harsh over the wind. "Jey, stop for a minute."

Jey stopped. She realized with a mild sense of despair that she was no longer anxious. Her heart rate had stabilized. Her mind had taken on the steady clarity it always did when she knew she was about to fight. She touched the long knives at her hips and ran her mind along her connection with Phril. He was gnawing on a brillbane husk, somewhere far away. It was convenient, she couldn't help but think, to have him out of danger.

"Jey." Lokim spoke her name firmly, as if trying to get her attention. She realized she'd turned to look back through the trunks. The orchard was a horrible place for a fight, but if the hounds found them here, this is where she would meet the hounds and kill them.

"Jey, look at me."

She turned to Lokim. His features were lost in shadow, but there was an intensity about the way he was staring at her. "Elle said you'd never heard of a passive barrier spell before. Was that true?"

Jey gave a small, unhappy nod. Although she was almost to the point of trusting Lokim, she still didn't like admitting any weakness.

Lokim's cloak blew and flapped, swirling around both him and Elle. Elle was still silent, still disconnected in the vague haze of over extension. "I think a passive barrier spell would contain our scent," he said. "But we won't know until we try."

◈

Elle seemed to be coming around a little. Lokim had taken his arm from around her shoulders, the better to concentrate on his spellwork. Jey led her now, holding her friend's cool, slender hand and doing her best to guide her over the rough terrain.

They'd left the orchard and moved into the forest, doubling back to head south and skirt the edge of Deramor. They'd changed directions several times – Lokim's compulsion to not walk straight to his hideout, Jey supposed.

Lokim's face was strained and pale. He strode ahead of them, leading the way. It had been at least fifteen minutes since he'd taken up the passive barrier spell. Jey could feel it around them, a light electricity on the air. And it seemed to be working. A bare minute or two after he'd cast the spell, the night had erupted with the voices of the frustrated hounds.

It seemed they'd lost the trail. For now, anyway.

Lokim, however, was growing tired. Passive spells weren't as taxing as active ones, but holding them for long periods of time was exhausting. Elle was still out of it, which left it to Jey to watch the night for signs of danger. She found herself missing Phril. Far away on his brillbane bush, he was aware of her anxiety but not enough bothered by it to come back and check on her.

If he'd been with her, he'd have been wild with rage and energy, ready to fling himself into the face of any foe. He would have been a liability, of course, but one that would have boosted her spirits a bit.

Up ahead, Lokim stopped. Jey stopped too, pressing Elle's hand to keep her from blundering into the young man's back. It was darker in the forest. A scrim of clouds had blown in to cover the moon. Jey could make out the outlines of trees and the bulk of a hill rising before them.

There was a grunt and a scrape, the grinding sound of stone on stone. Lokim's voice spoke out of the darkness. "In here," he said. "Go ahead. I'll close it behind us."

Jey strained her eyes to see, moving a few steps towards the hump of the hill. She could just make out an even blacker outline – a doorway leading into the hillside.

Off in the orchard, the dogs had quieted. Which meant they'd either picked up the trail or been called off. But even if Lokim's spell had neutralized the scent hounds, they were not safe. There were still the orderlies with their stunrods, the sight hounds, and, most dangerous of all, the other students.

Their situation was urgent, if not quite as desperate. Still, as Jey stared at the dark opening in the hillside, her calm evaporated. She felt a sudden fear sweep over her. Her heart seemed to constrict. Her mouth went dry. Her hand was slick where her palm rested against Elle's.

The fitful wind went still. Off in the woods, far in the distance, a man's voice called out. Another answered. Jey turned to look but could see nothing in the dim moonlight. The wind picked up again.

"Jey," Lokim hissed. "Come on." He reached forward and took Elle's other hand. Jey's friend moved without protest when guided, heading for the hillside.

As Elle stepped ahead, she gave Jey's hand a little tug. Jey experienced a sudden, intense desire to rip her hand from Elle's grasp and run. She was abruptly certain this was all an elaborate setup. Lokim had been grooming them, orchestrating his every move to bring about this moment – the moment he led her straight into a trap. He already had Phril, after all.

There was a curse in the darkness. Jey felt the rush of Phril's emotions as her tessila burst through the stitchring and came into near proximity again. His presence washed over her like an invigorating wave, pouring new energy into her body, heightening her senses.

There was a brief moment of confusion as the agitated tessila tangled in Lokim's shirt on his way out of the stitchring. But he fought his way free of the fabric and shot through the air to Jey. He burrowed himself into the scant space between her cloak and her neck, pressing his cool scales against her skin.

Lokim had not tried to stop Phril going to Jey. Her vision sharper, Jey could see him standing there by the hillside, his face creased with strain. He was still holding the passive barrier spell but there was a sheen of sweat on his forehead and his chest rose and fell with heavy respiration.

Elle, held between them, seemed to dawn into full awareness for the first time since they'd begun their flight. She looked at Lokim, blinking. "What's happening?" she said.

"We need to get inside," Lokim said in a flat, exhausted tone. "And your friend has once again decided I'm the enemy."

Elle gently pulled her hand free of Lokim's grip, then Jey's. She caught the flapping edges of her cloak and wrapped the garment around herself. She turned to look at Jey. She said, "I trust him."

Then she moved forward and disappeared into the hillside.

Jey felt a strange sting over her heart – as if an invisible dagger had pierced the skin there. Lokim still stood, waiting.

I can't leave Elle, Jey thought. But even as she thought it, she knew it wasn't true. If Elle had just walked into a trap, her only chance of ever getting out again was for Jey to remain free.

The wind died again and the forest went still. Into the quiet, Lokim said, "I can't wait any longer."

From the tunnel, Elle's voice came back, full of exasperation. "Jey, get in here."

With a low cry of terror and defeat, Jey hurried into the hillside.

CHAPTER 5

"She had it worse than I did, you know."

Jey heard the words as she drifted up out of sleep. It was Elle speaking, her voice low, something in it a little bit apologetic.

"You were in the same place, were you not?" Lokim's answer was also low. There was an intimacy to their tone, a snugness – as if they believed they were the only two people in the world.

Their voices came from nearby. Jey's training, kicking in to control her as usual, told her not to move, not to betray the fact she was awake.

Phril was also there. He'd refused Lokim's offer to go back through the stitchring after they'd settled in the hideout. The tiny animal was awake now, sitting on her shoulder like a sentinel.

Elle's voice had gone a little sadder when she replied. "I was trained primarily for diplomatic use. My strength is in the passive spellworks. I'm good at mental manipulations. I was used lightly – usually sent to parties or court functions. I had a whole fictional identity, did you know? There was a double who lived in town and pretended to be me. I was briefed each day on her activities so I could step in and be her whenever necessary. I don't think Jey even knows that."

Jey hadn't known. She felt an unpleasant shock of surprise. She had to repress a small surge of jealousy that Elle would tell Lokim something she hadn't confided in Jey. With the emotion came a desire to move and stretch, to banish the stiffness of sleep from her limbs. Jey repressed that as well.

It was quiet in the shelter, which had proven to be a long, low room buried deep in the hillside. Lokim said it was one of several such places near Deramor. They had been used to conceal and house refugees during the Betrayal. He'd known this place was here, but it had taken him weeks of searching to find a way in. There was a small spring in back that provided fresh water, and four different hidden entrances.

It was not a trap. It was a dusty, unused space that had been created to help desperate people – people who had once been in the exact same perilous position as Jey and Elle were now.

"So what did Jey do?" Lokim's voice was a teeny bit more clear, as if he'd turned to look at Jey as he spoke. Jey felt Phril stiffen on her shoulder, arching his neck and releasing a little hiss. Phril was convinced Lokim had done something to make Jey so afraid, which had inflamed all the tessila's protective instincts. Now the tiny creature was making his revised opinion of the young man clear.

"She was an assassin, mostly," Elle said. "And she used passive persuasion in places that were hard to get into. She can sneak into anywhere undetected, if she's alone. She was by far the most valuable of the three of us. She went on two or three times as many opportunities as me and Kae. Which means more drugs, more shots, more confusion. You can't blame her for not trusting you, Lokim. We've never been able to trust anyone."

There was a pause. Jey thought the conversation might turn. But Lokim spoke again, his voice was tight with contained anger. "They're letters," he said, putting it together. "J. K. L. They aren't even proper names." He seemed outraged at the thought. "Why do you still use them?"

Elle, unruffled, gave a little sigh. "L134," she agreed. "That's me." She laughed, but the sound contained no mirth. "What else should I call myself, Lokim? I don't remember my parents, much less the name they gave me."

If it was still windy outside, there was no way to know. They were surrounded on every side by several feet of solid earth. Lokim had lit a fire when they arrived. He'd built it on a hearth made of glittering red stones and heat had radiated throughout the room with surprising speed. Now the air was pleasant – not hot, not cold.

"What about Jey?"

Elle's tone carried a quiet sadness. "I don't think she knows any more than I do. But it's not something we talk about, you know?"

Lokim was quiet for a time as he considered this. "And your other friend? Kae? Did she decide to strike out on her own?" Lokim's voice had returned to its normal tone. There was a rustling sound as he shifted within his cloak.

Elle was still for a moment before answering. "She died. The night we escaped. I don't know what they used Kae for, but she was always so angry. Her tessila got too near one of our handlers. He killed it."

Another beat of silence, then Lokim said, "Your handlers were trained warriors as well, then?"

Elle laughed. There was another rustle of fabric in the still room. "Hardy. Nylan was a scholar, I guess. A sort of scientist diplomat who sent us on our opportunities. He knocked Kae's tessila out of the air and stomped on it."

This statement was followed by the longest silence yet. There was more rustling and movement and the scrape of a log set on the fire. Jey felt an immediate bloom of warmth beneath her. The stones she'd slept on had a softness to them. They were heated as well. She was growing a little too warm. She resisted another urge to move, to push aside her cloak and sit up to stretch her limbs.

"Stomped on it?" Lokim said. His tone was sad and wondering, and also there was a sort of understanding in it. "So your tessili," he said. "They don't know how to fight?"

Lokim's shelter was larger than Elle had expected. When he'd mentioned it before, she'd pictured a cave or a hollow behind a tree – some small space he'd carved out for himself in the wilds. Or perhaps the attic of an abandoned building, or a barn way out in some farmer's field.

She'd never imagined anything like the reality.

The place Lokim called his shelter was the most amazing space Elle had ever seen. While its shape was unassuming—a long, domed room hidden under a hill—the details of its construction took her breath away.

They'd made it here late the previous night. Jey had insisted on sitting up to keep watch. Lokim had tried to persuade her doing so was unnecessary as he'd gotten the fire started, but the light-haired girl had become so bristly and Lokim had been so exhausted, Elle had seen him give up and throw himself down into his cloak to sleep. Elle had done the same, falling into a deep slumber without taking much stock of her surroundings.

So when natural morning light had woken her, she'd come out of her sleep quickly, full of confusion. She'd opened her eyes and sat up, blinking in awe. The room around her had been full of sunlight. It streamed down from above as if through massive windows. But the ceiling in this place, Elle knew, was solid. It had to be. They were deep underground. If there had been windows, their fire the night before would have given them away.

"Sunstone." Lokim had spoken the word from his bedroll, his voice rough with recent sleep. "Have you never seen it before?"

Elle had shaken her head, sitting up and sifting through her pack until she found her hairbrush. As she combed and re-braided her hair, Lokim told her about the remarkable chamber. It had been made by the Tessilari, before their strength had been broken by war. There was magic woven into the floor, the ceiling, the walls, the store rooms. It was a feat of magical engineering and ingenuity alike.

"The sunlight was crucial, of course, for the brillbane." Lokim had nodded towards the far wall. Elle had noticed the floor there transitioned from stone to earth. The twisted remains of brillbane bushes stood along the far wall. They were nothing more than withered trunks – long dead.

And that was the reality of the place. It was remarkable, but old. The floors were covered in grit and dust. No one had lived here for lifetimes.

They had talked for a while, then. It had been nice. Elle adored Jey more than anyone else in the world, of course, but she couldn't help but think her friend was being a little unfair to this young man. Jey's suspicion and innate distrust had always been a kind of silent barrier between Lokim and Elle. Now, in the morning light that filtered into this strange, abandoned chamber, they were able to talk a little more freely.

All that ended when Phril went berserk. Jey was still asleep, but her tessila was on her shoulder, watching Lokim and Elle with his glittering eyes.

Lokim and Elle were talking about the academy. Lokim said the tessili at the academy did not know how to fight. Apparently in an effort to prove Lokim wrong, Phril launched himself into the air, flinging himself across the room in a blind rage.

Lokim, surprised, raised a hand to protect his face from the tiny, attacking creature. Phril slammed into it, clawing and hissing as he tried to tear out Lokim's eyes.

"Phril," Jey cried, sitting up all at once, squinting as she blinked at the broad light in the surrounding room. "What do you think you're doing?"

Shai, who'd been off flying lazy loops around the large room, came darting back to Elle, suddenly full of confusion and anxiety.

But it was Bliz that was the real surprise. The orange tessila had been dozing on Lokim's knee, tired from all the casting the young man had done the night before. She woke up now and leapt into the air, ready to fly to her human's defense.

What happened next took Elle by surprise. Lokim opened his eyes. With a quiet curse he reversed his hand, turning it deftly to catch Phril between his fingers. Phril screamed in outrage, squirming and hissing as Lokim flowed to his feet.

Bliz, in the meantime, transformed. One second, she was like Phril and Shai – a tiny speck of color in the bright air. The next she was a hulking presence, as tall at the shoulders as the sighthounds the academy used, and much thicker. Her scaled hide was glorious and vivid, her build one of compact, efficient power.

Elle gasped in pure shock, climbing to her feet to stare. Jey had taken a few steps forward, expression outraged, when Lokim had taken hold of Phril. But now she was frozen, staring at the massive Bliz in complete shock.

Bliz was furious. When she'd expanded, she'd settled onto the floor. Now she scuttled towards Lokim. She moved with flowing, sinuous grace. Her shapely head was almost as large as Lokim's and her eyes were focused with pure hatred on the hand that held Phril.

Lokim placed his hand against his own heart, ignoring its squirming occupant. He spoke in a voice that rang through the large chamber. "Bliz, that's enough. He's half mad, can't you? He doesn't know what he's about, and he can't hurt me. You need to settle down."

Elle recognized the tone of mild exasperation in Lokim's voice. How often had she sounded nearly the same when addressing Shai?

But instead of ignoring Lokim's reprimand, as Shai always seem to ignore Elle, the orange tessila stopped her advance. Bliz released a disgruntled huff, but turned around with not further resistance. Elle continued to stare as the now massive animal wandered away towards the dead brillbane.

◈

"They can all do it, as far as I know." Lokim spoke thoughtfully, sitting on one of the stone stools near the fire pit. He was holding a steaming mug of soup, which Elle had handed to him after warming it on the fire. Jey held a similar mug between her own hands. Its warmth was comforting against her palms. Its earthy scent made her realize how hungry she was. "How big they get varies a lot, as well as how long they can stay in larger form. Bliz is on the small size of average." He'd lowered his voice for the last sentence, as if he didn't want his tessila to hear.

Bliz, however, appeared to be asleep. She'd returned to her smaller size as soon as Phril had settled down. She'd fallen back into slumber as if nothing had happened at all.

Phril, on the other hand, was still agitated. He clung to the inside of Jey's sleeve, seething with resentment and a strange, fiery desire Jey had never felt in him before. The words Lokim had spoken troubled her. *He's half mad.*

Jey knew Phril wasn't the most rational of creatures. But there was no such thing as a rational tessila. Was there?

"They used to get bigger," Lokim was saying. "Much bigger. There are stories of the most powerful of the Tessilari who could make their tessili as large as houses and ride on their backs in flight." He laughed, sounding self-conscious. "Those must be exaggerations."

Jey tried to imagine what Phril would look like if he was as large as a house. The thought filled her with a little shudder of trepidation. At that size, his tantrums would be a lot more dangerous.

She glanced at Elle. Her friend's face had taken on a similar look of surprised dismay.

Lokim paused to sip his soup, then continued. "No one knows why they're getting smaller, but most agree it is probably due to a lack of variety in the bloodlines. We were able to rescue so few tessili when we fled, all the ones in the valley go back to the same ancestors. That's one of the reasons everyone was so excited when I told them about you and the existence of even more tessili at the academy."

Lokim went quiet, his words trailing off in a way that suggested he'd said something he hadn't mean to let slip. Jey looked up instantly, staring across the low fire at him with sudden sharp attention. "Wait," she said. "People know about us? People other than you?"

Lokim's face had flushed underneath his smooth tan. He ran a hand through his hair and said in a low tone, "Jey, they're your people, too. Even if you don't realize that."

Jey felt that fear constrict her heart again – the fear of the trap, the fear of losing the freedom she'd so recently gained. It was joined, now, by the new fear – fear that there was something wrong with Phril, that his years around the flashnodes and holdstones had permanently damaged him in some way.

Jey stood up, staring around the chamber with frantic eyes. She realized she didn't know how to get out. Whatever passage Lokim had opened last night was closed. "Elle," she said in a tight whisper, "we need to go."

Lokim stood too, his face flushing deeper with some new emotion. "Go where?" he said. "Back out into the woods, so you can get hunted and chased and attacked? Back to the cheesery, so you can endanger more innocent lives? Jey, I'm here to help you."

His voice rang with frustrated sincerity, but Jey hardly heard him. She went to her pack, collecting the few items she'd taken out the night before.

"Jey." It was Elle who spoke now. "I'm not going."

The words hit Jey like a blow across the back of the neck. She seemed to see stars. She straightened and turned.

Her friend was standing next to the fire, Shai hanging onto the end of her dark braid. Her eyes were large and sad. "I want to stop running," she said. "I'm tired. I'm afraid. We can't do this alone. We need help. I'm going with Lokim, back to meet the Tessilari. Maybe in the Valley of Mist, I can have a normal life."

The words sank in slowly. Jey closed her eyes. The terror still sang in her veins, frantic as a caged tessila. Her thought seemed to bunch and strain. *A normal life.* She almost laughed. Was that even possible for someone like her? *Maybe Phril's not the only one who's crazy.*

Jey spoke then, her words heavy and slow. "What do you remember, Elle? From the time before Professor Liam told me to cast that spell on Phril?"

Elle's face got that distant look it tended to assume when she was trying to draw on the past. Her narrow shoulders moved in a small shrug. "Opportunities, mostly. Dances and balls, state dinners."

"Exactly," Jey hissed. "Opportunities. That was the one time our brains were free of drugs, able to access what they knew and store thoughts and ideas for later."

Elle's face had gone a shade paler. She seemed to understand what Jey was getting at. "So all you can recall …" she said.

Jey slumped down against the wall of the shelter. The frantic energy drained out of her. "Killing," she said. "Killing and killing and killing."

Silence reigned for a long time. At last, Lokim spoke. "My people have sent out a small delegation – a sort of welcoming party. They want to meet you, to speak with you, to see your tessili. And, if you want, they'll see you back to the Valley of Mist. It's your choice, Jey, but there are people there, people in the valley, who have done nothing but study tessili their whole lives. If anyone can help you and Phril, it's the Tessilari."

Nylan shifted on the small wooden seat, his bad leg propped out before him. His cane leaned next to the folding chair. As he sat, the knee throbbed – a constant, irritating discomfort. He'd been walking too much the last few days out in the damp cold of the forest, tracking the two cursed students who had somehow stayed one step ahead of him for months.

It was a chilly, humid day with a half-frozen rain-mist drifting down through the trees. Nylan, huddled as he was within his cloak, was cold. He was cold and he was tired and his knee pained him. But he wasn't thinking about any of that.

What he was thinking about was victory. He was close, now. He knew it. The students had gone to ground in a hill. He didn't understand how they'd done it, but after a day of sweeping the area after the trail had vanished in the orchard, all signs pointed here. For the last three days his orderlies and guards, as well as at least one junior or senior student at all times, had watched this hillside with instructions not to intervene. They'd seen J114 twice, slipping out of the hillside to hunt and return. She seemed to have a found a way to diminish her scent trail to the point the hounds could barely follow it. But it also seemed she did so at the trade-off of invisibility. He'd left instructions she be allowed to move freely, that his men and students stay hidden.

Now, the trap was set. It was time for Nylan to turn the tables and reclaim the valuable property the academy had lost. J114 would be recaptured, if possible. She was too talented, too useful to not try, at least, to subdue and deploy a few more times. The other, L134, was expendable and would be killed on sight.

Nylan was confident he would catch them now. He was confident because he had a new weapon.

It sat next to his cane, similar in length and shape, though a good deal thicker. It was made of some kind of carved stone, with a handle at the top like a sword. The academy owned about a dozen of these implements, though the secret of their use had been lost at some point. For years they'd hung in the back of the hall where the orderlies met, gathering dust.

After the breakout at the academy, Nylan and devoted himself to reading, to researching ways to subdue and capture a Tessilari – for that is what these girls were. They were a fledgling version of those ancient warriors who'd once nearly toppled the kingdom.

His research had led him to these wands. It had taken him weeks of guessing and fiddling and failure after failure, but at last, he'd figuring out how they worked.

Now, he knew. It was simple. The weapon only needed to be charged by sticking the sharp tip into the earth for several hours. Then it could be deployed by setting the end on the ground and twisting the handle up top. It would send out a stunning ripple of magic, disabling any tessili or human bound to one, within a fifteen foot radius.

It was a glorious find. Nylan had tested it on every student at the academy. None had been able to withstand its pulse. Orderlies were deployed around the hill now, six of them, each with one of these rods.

All was in readiness. They had only to wait for the inevitable moment when J114 came near.

Nylan rubbed his knee, a grim smile turning up the corners of his mouth. He was very much looking forward to making her regret the fact she'd ever defied him in the first place.

CHAPTER 6

They'd spent a good deal of time cleaning up the shelter. Elle had found a door to a sealed storeroom which had contained a stock of tools. They'd taken brooms to the dust-covered floor and rags to the bas relief carvings that wrapped the hall at eye level. These, once clean, gave off a faint glow when a fire was lit. The small figures that occupied the carved landscapes seemed to move in the shifting light. Jey had taken on the task of polishing them because it seemed endless. She needed something to keep her busy.

They were waiting. Lokim said the Tessilari would arrive any day. Jey had made her peace with their coming. She'd familiarized herself with all of the ways out of the hillside and could work the small spell that opened and closed the door hatches. Lokim had also taught them the passive barrier spell he'd used to throw the hounds off their trail. It was simple – similar to a passive shield but focused on forming a block to contain light and sound and air instead of magic.

So, the space was clean and Jey felt safe enough. But she was not comfortable. Neither were Elle and Lokim. She could read it in the stiffness of their bodies, the quick way they would put on a forced smile every time she made eye contact.

They weren't comfortable because they did not agree. Jey was willing to meet the Tessilari, but the Valley of Mist sounded too much like a more benign version of the academy. Once there, she would not be able to leave of her own volition. Once there, she would be subject to the laws and norms of a society she'd had no part in creating.

Once there, she'd no longer be free.

Jey took a break from her rubbing to untie her hair and tie it back again. She stretched her back and looked around the hall. The space had a cozy feel, in spite of its vast size. It would be a fine place to stay for a time. They were safe and sheltered. They had only to slip out a few times a week to hunt or purchase supplies in town. With Lokim's stitchring they wouldn't need to go back to the academy for brillbane.

It was a workable way to live, Jey thought. The problem was, Elle and Lokim were not on board.

Jey sighed, dropped her rag by the wall, and glanced up at the glowing ceiling. It had been a dreary day, but the clouds were shifting and the sun was thinking about peeking through. Now would be a good time to hunt. She strode to the corner where she kept her things. She strapped on her gear belt, swung her cloak around her shoulders, and approached the place where Lokim sat by the fire. He appeared to be writing something. Elle was off in the bath chamber, where the water in a still pool had grown warm after several days with the fire lit.

Lokim looked up as Jey approached, setting his leather tablet aside. Jey thought he looked thinner than when she'd first seen him. There were bruised half-moons under his eyes. Jey wondered if he hadn't been sleeping well.

"I'm going out hunting." Jey spoke the words in a low tone. There was something about this place that seemed to require stillness, careful movement, and low voices. "Phril is dozing. If you don't mind keeping him with you, it will make my job a little easier."

Phril and Shai, still thrilled to have brillbane bushes again, had continued to spend large chunks of time on the other side of the stitchring. They were both looking a good deal healthier.

Still, Jey's feelings towards Phril had shifted slightly in recent days. She would always love the little tessila, but now she couldn't help but see his behavior as a bit alarming and unbalanced at times. Lokim's words seemed to echo in her mind every time she looked at him. *He's half mad.*

The expression on Lokim's face indicated he was not thrilled with Jey's plan to hunt. On the other hand, they were low on food – largely due to Lokim himself. Jey had discovered after her first hunt that male humans eat approximately twice as much as female ones. And she suspected, looking at him, he'd not been eating as much as he needed since he'd been with them.

Lokim looked up at Jey. Something in his eyes made her wait a moment. There was strain on his face, as if he was on the verge of making some difficult decision. At last he dropped his eyes and stooped to reach into a side pocket of his pack. He pulled something free, sat up, and extended his hand towards Jey.

On Lokim's broad palm lay a stitchring. Jey blinked, glancing to the side to confirm that the ring Phril had passed through a few hours before was still in place around Lokim's neck. It hung on the outside of his shirt and vest so the tessili could return freely if they chose.

Lokim seemed to see the confusion on her face. "It's my spare. Take it."

She took it. The thin silver was cool against her skin. The chain slithered through her fingers as the ring passed from Lokim's hands to hers.

Lokim let his hand fall back to his side. "Now you only have to go with us if that's truly what you want."

Jey felt something go very still inside of her. She bent her head forward and hung the ring around her own neck, tucking it beneath her shirt so it was hidden. She and Lokim looked at each other, their eyes holding steady for several heartbeats.

Jey understood.

He was taking Elle, but he was giving her independence. He was doing that, even though he could have taken Elle without giving Jey anything at all.

"Thank you." Jey spoke the words into the quiet room. Then she turned and walked towards the exit.

◈

Lokim tried to return to his missive after Jey left, but it was no use. He was distracted now, uncertain he'd made the right choice. Jey was a liability. If he couldn't get her back to the Valley of Mist she would be loose in the world, and she would know about the remnants of the Tessilari. Even worse, if recaptured, she herself could be converted into a terrifying weapon and deployed against them.

Still, Lokim couldn't blame her for not wanting to go to the valley. To pretend he didn't understand her hesitation would be a bare lie. Had he not spent his entire life dreaming of what lay beyond the mists? Had he not defied his entire society, put all his people at risk, just to satisfy his own curiosity and wanderlust?

He'd left, in spite of all the people who'd asked him to stay. And he'd been labeled rogue because of it. He'd intended to spend a good deal more time out in the world before thinking about returning to his homeland.

A soft step sounded at the end of the long room. Elle moved into view. Her feet were bare and the throat of her shirt was unlaced to reveal the smooth, pale skin of her throat.

Like Jey, Elle had changed into her hunting leathers as soon as they'd reached the shelter, discarding the heavy, cumbersome dresses they'd worn in their haste to leave the cheesery. Now she walked with a lithe lightness of step that made Lokim forget to breathe.

Elle smiled when she saw Lokim looking at her. There was a total, disarming innocence to the smile. Lokim smiled back, wondering how a person could be so strong and so vulnerable all at once. He'd gathered through his attempts to flirt with Elle that she lacked any understanding of romance. This knowledge made him more hesitant than he might have been anyway. He also couldn't help but remind himself from time to time that she was a master at passive persuasion and could manipulate him into feeling any way at all about her.

Whatever was between them was a tenuous thing – a fledgling attraction that made Lokim's heart thunder any time she came near. Every time he looked at her, he found himself wanting nothing more than to get her back to the valley so she could be safe and they could have time to figure each other out.

The irony of the situation didn't escape Lokim. There would be a reckoning when he returned. He would have to make reparations. Some of the Tessilari might never forgive him, might never accept him back into society.

But that didn't matter. What mattered was getting Elle away from this world where she was a thing to be hunted, used, and discarded.

"That bath is amazing," Elle said as she lowered herself onto the stone stool next to him.

Her hair was damp. The scent it gave off convinced Lokim he'd get no more of his account written today. He stowed his tablet and scribis and turned to face Elle. "I hope it helped you relax a little."

For a moment, he couldn't help but realize Elle had been bathing alone moments before, up to her chin in warm water. And he'd been staring at a cursed leather tablet.

His face beginning to flush, Lokim hurried to add, "Jey went out hunting."

As he spoke the words, there was a stirring in the spell that powered the stitchring. There was something sharp about the feeling – which meant a tessila was about to come through was in a hurry. Lokim sat up straight and clamped both hands around the silver ring.

Phril blasted into his fingers in full fury. Jey's tessila exploded through the ring, met the barrier of Lokim's hands, and began to claw and bite with such anger Lokim almost let him go. He gritted his teeth and restrained the small animal, shifting his grip so the tessila's head was free and the legs, with the small but raking claws, were pinned against the animal's body.

Phril writhed and flailed, flinging his head from side to side in irrational combat. Lokim watched the animal struggle with a sick feeling of dismay. All tessili were passionate, but Phril and Shai seemed different, somehow – as if they'd had the ability to reason entirely removed from their minds.

Elle was staring at the struggling Phril with wide-eyed concern. "Jey," she murmured. She rose, buttoning up her shirt and slipping into her leather vest.

She was swinging her weapons belt around her hips when Lokim spoke. "No," he said. "I'll go." He rose, extending the hand holding Phril towards Elle. "You hold onto him."

It was absurd, he knew. Lokim had passable skill as a hunter, but he was no trained fighter like Elle was. Still, the thought of her going out to see what had befallen Jey made him sick. He took the stitchring from around his neck and placed it around Elle's. Then he hurried across the large chamber towards the exit before she had a chance to argue.

◈

Elle stared down at the frantic Phril with a distinct feeling of unease. She heard the grind of the stone portal, a pause, then more grinding. Which meant Lokim was gone.

She wasn't sure why she'd let him intercede like that. She was, after all, Jey's best friend. She and Jey had stood together since the day Jey had cast the spell on Shai that had allowed Elle to remember.

Thinking about that now, Elle felt a slow bloom of guilt spread through her stomach. During one of their long, quiet talks by the fireside, Elle had told Lokim she and Jey had escaped together. But that wasn't true. Deep down, Elle knew Jey had been solely responsible for their breakout of the academy. Jey was the one who'd learned to shield tessili from the flashnodes. Jey was the one who'd coached Elle and Kae through the days that followed, learning to blend in at the academy in spite of being able to form new memories. But most importantly, Jey had stolen the syringe from Nylan, used it on herself, and then shown Elle and Kae how to blast the drugs from their own veins.

That didn't begin to consider all the times Jey had saved them both since then – the hunting, the fighting, the hiding.

And now Elle had threatened to abandon her one true friend for a man she hardly knew.

Phril, as if reading her thoughts, gave a resentful hiss and heaved against her hold on him. She brought her attention back to the moment. She dared not let him escape. The little tessila would batter himself to death trying to leave this place to get to Jey.

Elle sighed and paced around the fire, Lokim's stitchring glittering against her dark vest. Having seen Bliz expand to the size of a large hound, Elle now understood the protective instincts of the tessili a bit better. Always before, she'd found Shai's evident desire to battle all foes endearing, if a bit inconvenient and perplexing. Now she thought of it differently.

There was a strange shift in the air. Elle paused and frowned, looking around. Then Shai burst through the stitchring. Elle gasped as the spell on the ring drew from her to power itself. The room around her wavered. She collapsed to her knees. She was suddenly woozy with exhaustion. The large hall seemed to dissolve into gray squares. She seemed to lose herself.

When her vision cleared, Elle found herself kneeling by the fire, her palms flat against the cool stone of the chamber floor. Her heart was hammering and there was a sheen of sweat on her forehead. As she pushed herself to her feet, she remembered the strain she'd seen on Lokim's face that first night all three tessili had gone through the stitchring. Had it been taking this much from him every time they'd used it? If so, Elle couldn't believe he was still on his feet.

Elle dusted off her palms, noticing a small scratch on her finger. She raised her hand to stare at it, looking at the bead of blood on the base of her thumb with a sense of confusion that dawned into horror. "Phril," she gasped, staring around the chamber in frantic concern.

She couldn't see the red tessila, but Shai was there, darting about her head in frantic circles.

Elle knew what she had to do. She ran towards the door Lokim and Jey had gone through a few moments before. Releasing Phril into the world was a risk, but trapping him inside this place would lead to his certain and immediate death. "Find Phril," she said to Shai. "Bring him to the door. I'll open it." Then she darted across the hall, feet still bare, hoping her tessila could do what she asked.

◈

Something was very wrong.

Jey seemed to wake up. There was a pain in her head and another in her side and another in her shoulders. Those pains were dull. There was also a burning hot pain in her calf.

Behind the pain, there was a dullness to her mind – a kind of sluggish, stiffness she struggled against to no avail.

And beyond all that, there was anger.

Jey stirred, trying to sort out the sensations. There was a gritty, cold dampness against her cheek.

She was lying on the ground.

And the anger. It seemed to roil through her like an inferno, so hot it burned her mind. It wasn't her anger, she understood. It was Phril's.

The thought of her tessila seemed to bring clarity to Jey's mind. She couldn't see because she was lying all but face down. Jey tried to move, to bring an arm up and push herself into a sitting position. She could not. When she tried to move her arm she felt a chafing sensation around her wrists.

She was bound.

Jey didn't struggle against the bonds. She rolled over instead. She blinked as the wan sunlight of the afternoon filled her eyes. She heard someone say, "Oh. Excellent. She's come around already. Help her sit up, won't you, Donin."

Jey recognized the voice. It sent terror racing up and down her limbs.

Nylan. It was High Handler Nylan.

A hard hand closed around Jey's shoulder. She was hauled into a sitting position and heaved around so her back was propped against the rough trunk of a tree. Jey blinked. Her head felt wobbly on her neck. Phril's anger was a distracting buzz beneath her thoughts but she managed to focus her vision.

She was in the woods, not far from the shelter. And she saw two things that made her very scared. First, Nylan stood before her, leaning on a strange stone cane. Second, Lokim lay nearby, bound as she was, unconscious.

There was no sign of Phril or Bliz. Jey stared at Lokim long enough to determine his chest still rose and fell with his breath.

Jey relaxed by a small fraction. She glanced about the woods. Elle was not in evidence, a fact she hoped was a good sign.

That was about where the good news ended, though. At the edge of her peripheral vision, Jey saw two orderlies, stunrods held at the ready.

"I want to know how you did it."

Jey turned her head at the sound of Nylan's voice. The man stood a little distance away and he was looking at her. Something in his eyes made Jey flinch. The rage she saw there was a match for the boiling fury Phril was feeling. It was unnerving to see that emotion in the face of a human.

Nylan's face had never been kind, but now there was a brutal twist to his features. He took a couple steps forward. Jey saw he walked with a pronounced limp. He moved closer but stopped before he was anywhere near Jey's reach. "How did you escape? How did you get your little monsters past the magic? If you tell me without fighting, perhaps I'll spare your lover's life."

Jey's mind was still hazy. For a moment, she didn't understand what he meant. Then, she blinked and glanced at Lokim. The young man lay unconscious, his dark hair shifting in the afternoon breeze. Nylan, she realized, must think Lokim was a normal young man, someone whom Jey had grown attached to.

Well, that was also good. The longer it took for Nylan to figure out Lokim was Tessilari, the better his chance of survival.

Jey swallowed and discreetly tested her bonds. The rope on her wrists was tight. There were bonds on her ankles, as well. She could blast them off with a spell, but the orderlies with the stunrods would whack her before she could escape. She could try to hit Nylan with an offensive spell, but then, too, the orderlies would club her senseless before she could do him any real harm. And then they'd be right back in this same spot, only Nylan would be angrier.

Nylan was watching her, his face growing more grim with every second she remained silent. "Jorin," he said, tone hard, "why don't you see if you can wake the young man up."

Grinning, a man stepped up from behind Nylan, drawing a knife from his belt.

He was walking towards Lokim when Phril arrived.

At first, the red tessila was nothing more than a red glint on the air. Jey saw him with a strange twist of her heart. "No," she whispered. He was so small. She remembered, vividly, the smashed body of Kae's tessila, stomped into the ground and dead.

Phril shot past the tree Jey was leaning against, and looped around the trunk in one quick circle. She felt him take stock of her and reassure himself she wasn't too badly harmed. Then she felt his focus shift onto Nylan.

From there, everything happened almost too quickly to follow. One of the orderlies shouted a warning. Nylan turned, saw the red tessila, and grinned. He pulled a stunrod from his belt.

Then, in the instant between when he flew past Jey and reached Nylan, Phril changed. His body shimmered and seemed to expand. His new, larger shape was translucent at first. Then it solidified. Only now, Jey's tessila was the size of horse.

The suddenly massive red tessila hit Nylan like a speeding carriage. The man had time to let out a cry of surprise before a single swipe of a great forearm batted him aside with no more effort than a cat tosses a mouse into the air. Nylan was flung away to smash into a tree and slide to the ground, groaning.

There was a moment of stunned silence. Phril raised his head to the sky. He let out an ear-splitting roar, its reverberations shaking the very earth. Jey felt a strange swelling pride at the sight of him. He was magnificent. His hide glittered in the sun. His head was fine and intelligent. And he was hers.

Then, the first arrow pierced Phril's gleaming hide.

◈

The arrows hit Phril's scaled hide with deep, hard thumps. Jey felt his pain lace through her own body. She gasped with the shock of it. Phril wheeled, glaring around the trees. But he was a large target and the archers were well hidden. More arrows found him even as he spun.

Jey heard shouts behind her and the scuff of fleeing feet. Phril, hearing the same sounds, turned on the orderlies that had been standing over Jey and were now running away. He thundered forward only to crash against a tree trunk, causing a shower of twigs and leaves to fall onto Jey's head. She could feel his confusion at the size of his body combined with his anger at what had happened to her. But it took only a moment before he recovered from the crash with the tree and lit off after the orderlies.

Which left Jey alone with the groaning Nylan and the unconscious Lokim.

Mind racing, Jey cast a passive echo spell on herself. Then she turned her attention to her bonds. She focused, beginning to weave a spell. Before she could release it she heard running footsteps. She turned to see two young women dressed in dark leather. They ran forward, holding crossbows. One of them went to Nylan, stooping over his crumpled form. Jey heard him hiss some order. The girl straightened and spoke to her companion. "He says to get her back to the academy."

The girls turned as one and took a step towards Jey. Jey felt a strike on her passive echo spell – a magical missile that caused pain to lance through her mind. She cursed and targeted the bonds on her feet with an active strike spell, but it glanced off the rope and hit the damp loam of the forest floor, where it sizzled. Nylan, always thorough, had used magically resistant rope.

The two students moved forward. Jey felt another strike against her shield. It was all too much. Phril's pain and rage sang in her mind. The painful spot on her calf seemed to be growing more uncomfortable by the minute. She glanced down to see her legging was punctured, the leather around it dark with blood. Nylan must have stubbed her in the leg when she'd been unconscious.

Somehow, the sight of her own blood was the last straw. Jey lost her hold on the passive echo spell. As soon as it fell the two girls moved forward in confident unison, preparing to grab her arms, heave her off the ground, and haul her back to the academy.

"No," Jey whispered. The word barely made it past her dry throat. In the distance she could here Phril crashing through the woods, bellowing in pain and rage. "Please," she said, addressing the two girls. "I can help you. I can show you how to escape. I can tell you the secret. You can gain your own freedom."

One of the two, a slim girl who looked like she couldn't be any older than 15, back-handed Jey across the mouth. The blow was hard, calculated, and it hurt. "No talking," the girl said. Then she stooped towards Jey's shoulder.

There was a blur in the air, the fuzzing pull of magic being worked nearby. Jey gasped as a staff seemed to appear out of thin air. It arced down towards the girl as the man swinging it dropped his passive echo spell and became visible.

He was a man unlike any Jey had ever seen. He was not as tall as Lokim, and he was a few years older. He wore a long coat the color of mist. His staff bore traceries of elaborate runes up and down its length. His face bore a look of grim determination. His jaw was set, his grip on his staff was firm, but he didn't look worried. He expected the slender girl to be an easy mark.

If the girl who had slapped Jey was at all surprised by the man's sudden appearance, she didn't show it. She spun, caught the staff in her hands, and jerked it from the man's grasp. He stumbled back, startled.

The girl reversed her grip and swung the staff back at its owner. It whistled through the air in a furious swipe, missing his head by a hair's breath. The second girl turned away from Jey, pulling her knives from her belt in an angry hiss.

The man cursed and began to weave another passive echo spell. The two girls attacked it before he could get the weave right, blasting it out of existence before it could settle into place.

The man's eyes widened with sudden fear. *They're going to kill him.* Jey's heart sank at the thought.

Jey felt a tug on her bonds. She looked down to see Bliz, about the size of a rabbit, gnawing busily through the rope on her legs. It took the tessila's sharp teeth only a moment to sheer through the rough fibers. Jey gasped with relief as her ankles came loose. She held out her hands. The tessila freed those as well.

"Thank you," she whispered, surging to her feet. Her weapons belt had been removed when she'd been tied, but she didn't hesitate. She ran forward to join the fight, limping on her wounded leg.

Jey didn't need weapons to be deadly.

CHAPTER 7

The girl with the knives turned as Jey approached. Her eyes narrowed as she took in Jey's battered appearance – her limp, her empty hands. As the man who'd lost his staff held one student at bay through magical jabs and blocks, Jey wove a passive shield around herself and dropped it into place. She steeled her mind against the pain in her leg, putting it aside to deal with later. Then she lunged forward.

The girl with the knives didn't hesitate. She swung one knife towards Jey's side, bringing it in low and quick. Jey wove an active strike spell and targeted her opponent's wrist. There was a shock on the air, a gasp from the girl. The knife fell free. Jey tumbled to the side to scoop it up the moment it hit the earth and came back to her feet in a roll.

She now had a knife. But behind her opponent the man in the coat was losing ground. His face bore a bewildered expression and he stumbled backwards in a continuous retreat. He'd produced a small hunting knife which he held at ready, but it wasn't much use against the whirling, snapping staff.

Jey's opponent was cautious now. She held her one knife to the side and stalked Jey like a hunting cat. In the distance Jey could hear distant shouts, the excited barking of dogs, and the long, high whistle of the master of the hunt. She didn't have much time.

She parried a quick, vicious swipe of her opponent's knife and realized with sudden surprise Phril was no longer in pain. The only discomfort in her mind was her own. Her tessila, in fact, was feeling quite satisfied with himself. He was basking in some emotion – some feeling she couldn't quite identify.

Jey had no time to figure it out. She darted in to deliver an attack. The student blocked her strike, but Jey's blade slid off her opponent's hilt and sliced through the leather on her forearm. Blood flowed and the girl jumped back with a gasp. *So young. So inexperienced.* The thought made Jey sad.

She heard a shout from the man in the coat. She turned in time to see a ring of bright light erupt around him. It blasted out in a brilliant circle, knocking his attacker back a few paces. But it wasn't enough. The student recovered a moment later to stalk forward again.

Jey pressed her advantage, taking her opponent's momentary imbalance as the cue to move in. She blocked a knife swipe and felt her passive shield spell reverberate as it deflected a magical strike. Jey closed with the girl and dropped her own knife to catch the girl's wrist in both of her hands. She twisted. There was a pop and a cry, and the knife came free. Jey caught the knife, turned it, and brought it in with a vicious strike to the side of the girl's head.

The girl crumpled, collapsing into a heap on the forest floor. Jey turned and began to hobble towards the man in the long coat.

But even as she watched, she saw she would be too late. The man had gambled on the spell that had produced the light. He was tired now, his retreat slow and clumsy. The student pressed him with an unhurried deliberation that made Jey's blood run cold. The man stumbled on a rock, lurched to the side, and his back ran into a tree. The girl whirled the staff, preparing to bring it down across the man's face. Jey felt a sick horror rise to choke her throat. Whoever this man was, he had tried to help her. Would it cost him his life?

As Jey watched, too far away to help, the staff began to fall. The man saw it coming and raised one arm in a feeble block.

But just before the blow landed, Elle appeared, dropping a passive echo spell to erupt in the middle of the fight. Armed with her knives, she deflected the swing of the staff and delivered a quick cut to the student's shoulder before the girl could dance back.

Jey gave a short sigh of relief. She glanced around. Lokim was sitting up now, rubbing at his wrists and staring at Elle with a look of such unguarded admiration Jey had to look away. Bliz was perched on his shoulder, returned to her usual size.

She looked for Nylan, but the handler was gone.

A shout sounded from Jey's right. Three orderlies rushed her, charging out from behind a large bush, stunrods raised. Jey barely had time to look at their faces before they were upon her, swinging, cursing, trying to bring her down. She didn't recognize any of them. Which made it easier.

She caught the first one with a side swipe of her blade across the neck, dropping him. She rose up to meet the second, plunging upwards to bring her knife into his stomach and leave it there. The third balked as his comrades fell. She slashed his wrist, so the stunrod fell from his grip. Then she clubbed him with her pommel like she'd dropped the student.

Then Jey stopped. She was aware she was breathing hard, her blood singing in her veins. Abruptly, she understood the emotion she'd caught from Phril earlier.

It was the joy of the kill.

◈

Jey turned her back on the fallen orderlies, trying to ignore their groans. She tried to hurry forward, but the wound in her calf had grown harder to ignore. It throbbed with a bright, searing pain, sending spots to bloom over her vision and blot out the forest. Jey blinked, drew in a few deep breaths, and tried to focus.

Elle now faced the student alone. The man in the coat had disappeared. Elle was on the defensive, which was her preferred way to fight. She blocked and parried and took small steps backwards, waiting for a moment when she could dart in and deliver her own attack. Her knives clashed and rasped on the staff as it spun and whirled on the air.

There was a tug of magic. The strange man appeared beside Jey, kneeling. Jey jerked back from him in surprise as he extended a hand towards her leg, just stopping the reflex that told her to bring her hands down hard across the back of his skull.

The man glanced up at her. His face was drawn with fatigue, but he looked at her without fear. "You can't fight like this, and I am beaten." He gestured towards the oozing blood on her leg. His voice was smooth and low.

His eyes were a rich, honeyed brown that seemed bright even in the dim forest.

Without further explanation, the man clamped his hands around Jey's wounded calf. The touch was firm – just shy of hard. Jey gasped as pain lanced through her, so intense now she barely remained on her feet.

Nearby she heard the whack and whirl of the staff and Elle's small grunts of effort as she held the attacking student at bay. Further off, she heard the shuffle and tramp of moving feet. There would be more orderlies with stunrods, maybe more archers, probably hounds. They had to move.

The man bowed his head over his hands. "My name is Treyam." His tone seemed to suggest they had met in polite society rather than next to the bodies of three men Jey had just disabled. She noticed his tessila for the first time. She was peeping out of one of the wide sleeves of the coat. Her scales were a pale blue, her eyes glittering black.

Jey found herself answering in kind. "Treyam. Thank you. I'm Jey."

Then her leg was full of a different kind of heat. A fierce but somehow soft sensation bloomed from Treyam's hands, penetrating deep into the meat of her damaged calf. The warmth stayed and the pain ebbed.

A moment later, Treyam stood. He looked at her with eyes that were deeply weary. "Now," he said. "Go help your friend."

As Jey moved towards Elle and the student, she felt another surge of intense emotion from Phril. Simultaneously, there was a crash off in the woods, followed by a roar and a number of screams. Then she felt more pain from him, but also more of that hot, violent satisfaction. *Phril*, she thought. *Come back.*

He didn't seem to be aware of her desire for him to return. He was wild with anger, high on his new ability to change size. *What about the arrows?* But there wasn't time to worry about it. Elle needed help.

Jey jogged past Lokim, who'd tried to get to his feet several times only to fall back to the earth. Now he sat with a hand pressed to his forehead, looking bewildered.

There wasn't time to worry about that either. Jey continued forward, watching the fight as she approached. She saw what was taking so long. Elle was fighting – yes, defending herself against a younger, less skilled opponent. But Elle's conservative attacks showed she wanted to disarm the student, to disable her, but not do her harm. *Too soft-hearted.*

Watching them, Jey was filled with sudden anger. The girl from the academy was fighting with no such restraint. Elle had lost one knife and held her empty hand curled into a fist, the fingers purple in a rapidly spreading bruise.

Behind her, Jey heard low voices – Treyam speaking with Lokim. Jey moved quickly but smoothly, changing her trajectory each time the fight shifted, trying to approach without being seen.

Jey was a few steps away from engaging the student when a dog burst out of the woods, running at top speed. It was a sighthound – tall and lean, lips pulled back from its long teeth in a snarl. Jey could make out the shape of a man behind it, pointing at Elle.

Jey shouted, too far away to intercede. The dog flattened into a run, closing on her friend. The student, seeing her advantage, pressed her attack even harder.

There was a streak of red on the air – a tiny red blur. Phril appeared, zipping around a tree trunk, heading straight towards the attacking dog. He'd shifted back to his tiny size. Jey's heart all but seized at the sight of her miniscule tessili hurling himself towards the much larger hound. Had he forgotten he was small again?

Jey's advance faltered, her heart stuttering as her tiny tessila flew to the attack. *If he dies, I die.* The thought made her strangely cold.

But it didn't happen as she'd feared.

The instant before reaching the dog, Phril shimmered, expanded, and solidified. There was a massive crash as the tessila's sudden bulk and velocity met the dog's charge and broke it. The dog gave a yip. The two animals tumbled until they hit a tree. Then Phril picked the dog up in his jaws and flung it away into the woods.

The student who'd been fighting Elle faltered in her attack to glance towards the sight of the massive Phril, once again as large as a horse and now smeared with blood. Jey looked for the arrow wounds, but the scales of his neck were smooth and unblemished. He'd somehow healed himself.

Elle did not allow herself to be distracted. In that bare instant of opening, she stepped within the reach of the staff, blocking a clumsy, belated swipe. Elle didn't use her knife. She brought her empty hand to the girl's head and released a powerful blast of magic, scrambling the girl's wits and forcing her into unconsciousness.

The second student crumpled to the earth.

◈

"I don't understand." Jey spoke as she looked at Phril. The tessila was normal sized again, a small particle of color on the air. "He was shot. I saw him."

Lokim grunted, heaving a pack onto his back. Elle was nearby, stowing her last few belongings. They'd retreated into the shelter to gather their things and wait for the academy to congregate its forces around what they would now believe was the entrance to the hideout. Then they would slip out by another exit.

Lokim rubbed at his head, where he'd apparently taken a hard blow to the skull. He couldn't remember what had happened to him after leaving the shelter. He recalled waking to the sounds of fighting with Bliz gnawing through his bonds. He'd been unable to stand. There had been something wrong with his balance and he'd had a headache so fierce he'd been unable to keep his eyes open. "They heal when they change form," Lokim said. "It's what makes them so difficult to kill. Most of them can only shift once or twice a day. They have to be strategic about when they use the ability."

Jey tied her crossbow to the outside of her pack. Her forehead was creased with a small frown. "Phril is never strategic about anything." She glanced to the side as she spoke, eyes straying towards the dark form that lay on the far side of the hall – Treyam, wrapped in his coat, trying to steal a little bit of rest before they left to meet the other Tessilari. His sky blue tessila lay curled on his stomach, watching them with her glittering eyes.

Jey looked back at Lokim, propping her pack upright against her legs. "Bliz freed me first," she said. "She came to me, made herself large enough to gnaw through my bonds and set me free. You were right there next to me, unconscious. But she helped me."

Bliz was inside Lokim's collar now, drowsing against the warmth of his skin. He felt a deep affection for his clever, sweet tessila. "She could see freeing you would do the most good. Unconscious, I couldn't help myself, much less anyone else."

Jey's face seemed to darken again. Elle returned, moving from the storeroom where they'd stowed their food, her own pack bulging.

Jey spoke, something in her eyes sad. "Phril would never do anything so rational. For a moment there, I thought he was going to leave – to run off after the orderlies and refuse to stop until he'd killed them all." She seemed to tremble at the thought.

Lokim didn't let his own unease show. Phril, having just gained the ability to shift, was the largest tessila

Lokim had heard of in recent times. If he went berserk, it would be a disaster.

"They're all unique, Jey," he said, as if reassuring her could ease his own anxiety.

Jey's eyes seem to settle on the small blue tessila on Treyam's chest. "Where was she, during the fight? Phril was trying to kill everyone."

Lokim felt a pang of discomfort, brought on by old memories full of regret and nostalgia. "Nim is unusual," he said. As he spoke, Treyam stirred, shifting into a sitting position and blinking around with bleary eyes. Lokim dropped his voice to a lower register. "She's not aggressive." As Jey stared at him in stunned incomprehension, he added. "She doesn't fight or get angry. Ever."

There was the rustle of the long coat and the soft sound of steps as Treyam walked across the hall to join them. His eyes flicked over Lokim in that appraising way that had always made him feel exposed. "Time to get back to the valley," Treyam said.

Lokim looked at the man. He was exhausted – it showed in every line of his face, the stoop of his shoulders, the set of his jaw. He'd worked two major healings in a short span of time, not to mention all the magic he'd expended in his fight with the student. It was a wonder he was on his feet at all.

But then, Treyam had always been resilient.

Lokim looked aside, determined not to let the past affect the present. He touched the place on his skull again, where Treyam had healed him. He said, "Yes. We should go."

Jey walked through the forest, eyes on the terrain in front of her. As she moved she was aware of two remarkable things. First, her calf didn't pain her at all. Second, Phril was happy.

There was no other way to describe it. Feeling the echo of his emotion made her realize she'd never felt him this way before. She'd felt him content, yes, certainly, and excited or pleased or grateful.

But this. Happiness was something different. It was a warm emotion. It seemed to glow inside her, giving her strength and confidence.

She was walking behind Treyam, following the bobbing hem of his strange coat. Lokim and Elle were behind her, side by side. The three of them carried packs. And around them, holding in a precise formation and moving on silent feet, walked the Tessilari.

Treyam, it turned out, was an advanced scout from the party that had been sent to meet them. They'd slipped out of the shelter together, skirted the hunters in the woods, and joined up with his people.

The other Tessilari were a varied bunch. There hadn't been time for introductions. Behind, the whistles and bays had told them their foes were reorganizing. And Nylan was still with them.

Around her, Jey could feel the shimmer of magic. The Tessilari were holding two spells in place – a massive passive echo spell large enough to hide them all, and a passive barrier of the same size.

They were doing it collaboratively. Three Tessilari supported each spell. Jey could feel the way the weaves knit together, joining to form a protective dome far larger than any individual could have managed alone. It was a concept Jey had never considered before, and it stunned her – the idea that two people could share their magic.

The man, Treyam, stumbled stepping over a rock. Jey found herself stepping aside and coming up beside him as he regained his balance. His face still had that drawn look. He was exhausted, seeming hardly able to do anything beyond putting one foot in front of the other.

Jey, suspecting the wound in her own calf hade taken a lot out of him, felt the bite of guilt in her stomach. "Is there anything I can do to help you?"

Treyam glanced up as she spoke. Now that they were out of immediate danger, there was something light about his face – a sort of spark in his eyes and a turn of his mouth that suggested he was near smiling. His tessila rode on his shoulder now, dozing.

"Tell me how you taught your tessila to grow to such prodigious size." In spite of his exhaustion, his tone was playful.

But Jey found herself flushing. After he'd killed the dog, Phril had wanted to take off after the dog's handler. Jey had tried to tell him to stay, but he'd ignored her – so high on battle fever he'd been ready to defy her direct command. It had been Treyam's tessila who had stopped him, somehow, flying into his face and hissing, flaring her wings and lowering her head to stare into his battle maddened eyes.

Phril had gone still. A shudder had rippled through him. At last he'd shifted back to his tiny size and flown to Jey. He'd been sleeping in her sleeve ever since.

"Today was the first time he ever changed size." Jey said the words in a wondering tone. It seemed too much had happened for the short span of time that had passed since she'd gone out to hunt. There had been no discussion once they'd reached the Tessilari. Lokim had filled the leader in with a brief sketch of their circumstances. Then the party had moved out.

Now, Jey walked with them. She could feel the protective dome around them. The sounds of those who would hunt them were growing fainter, fading into the dim woods.

But although Phril was happy, Jey was not. With every step she took she felt a strange tug – a desire to go back, to find the two fallen girls, to tell them everything, to teach them how to escape the horrible life of slavery she'd left them to.

It wouldn't help. She knew that. The moment Nylan got those two back to the academy, he'd pump them so full of drugs they would forget everything.

"What troubles you?" This question came from Treyam. He'd been watching her face, Jey realized. She looked up to see sincerity in his amber eyes.

Jey glanced behind her. Lokim and Elle were moving together, Lokim always pausing if Elle slowed.

Elle was safe now. At least Jey had achieved that much.

"I need to go." Jey spoke the words, realization breaking in her mind, clear as the tree trunks around her. "I can't leave them. I need to go back. I need to destroy that place."

She stopped walking as she heard the truth in her own words. Around her, the Tessilari drifted to a halt. Jey realized she'd spoken louder than she'd meant to.

She glanced at Elle. Her friend's face carried an expression that was both sad and resigned. *She won't try to stop me.* The realization caught at Jey's heart a little, but she pushed it aside.

Jey raised her voice. "Thank you, all, for your help. But I need to go back." She took a step, moving away from Treyam, meaning to leave the protective circle of spellwork.

It was the leader who spoke. She was a middle-aged woman with silver streaked hair, gray eyes, and a brilliant green tessila. Her voice was firm but not hard. Her eyes were sharp, but not cruel. She said, "If you go now, you'll die alone. You will help no one."

The statement hadn't been said in a loud tone, but the shock of it settled like a weight across Jey's shoulders.

Her response came without thought, escaping her lips in barely more than a whisper. "Better that than not trying at all."

It was Treyam who answered this time. He had moved to stay near her. His tone was warm and gentle and full of sincerity. "If you come with us now, wait a while, form a plan – I'll go back with you when the time is right. We'll bring that place down together."

Jey glanced at the man in surprise. The look of laughter had faded from his face. His expression was hard, full of determination.

The woman spoke again. "There may not be many of us left in this world, but all of us are done being slaves, done seeing our people tortured and killed. We'll fight with you, if you give us a little time."

Jey turned in a circle, rotating to look at the faces of the Tessilari. They varied in age, eye color, hair color, height, gender, and the color of their tessili. But one thing was consistent.

Every single one of them looked sincere.

"Lokim has told us of the place you came from." The woman continued to speak, eyes never wavering as they looked at Jey. "It cannot be tolerated. We won't allow it to exist. If you go alone, you throw your life away. If you go with us, you can see the academy fall."

It was Phril who decided it for her. The tessila had woken when the swaying of Jey's sleeve had stopped. He stirred now, feeling a little thrill at the word "fall." Jey tried to remember if she'd ever felt him respond to an individual word that way.

She lifted her sleeve to look at her tessila. He blinked at her, his black eyes bright and clever as always. But there was something new behind them – some increased level of understanding.

Phril was changing. Since he'd been going through the stitchring with Bliz, he'd developed somehow, matured. If she went back now, back to the academy, she'd never know why.

Jey lowered her arm. She closed her eyes for one long moment. She remembered what Elle had said, the night Jey hadn't wanted to go into the hillside. *I trust him.*

Jey opened her eyes. Treyam was looking at her. There was warmth in his face again.

He extended a hand.

Maybe she couldn't trust the Tessilari. Maybe she couldn't trust anyone. Not yet.

This man had thrown himself into a fight to help her, stood against foes he didn't understand, then exhausted himself to heal her leg, all before even knowing who she was. Perhaps she could try to trust one man.

It was a place to start.

Jey reached out and set her hand in Treyam's.

Wordlessly, the Tessilari around her began to move forward again, away from Tessili Academy, towards the Valley of Mist.

Tessili Revenge

Chronicles of the Tessilari : Book III

Robin Stephen

First Mage Otha sat in her private greenhouse, chair oriented so the unbroken sunlight poured through the windows onto her face. Although the day was young and the dry wind outside carried a sharp edge as it blew down from the frosted peaks, here among the brillbane the air was warm.

Still, Otha had a woolen blanket spread across her lap. It seemed she was never quite warm anymore. She supposed such were the consequences of living for over 400 years.

There was a rustling near the entryway, and a murmur of voices. First Mage Otha suppressed a sigh. She had agreed, again, to meet with High Mage Agina, even though they both knew their conversation would doubtless play out in a manner no different from all the times before.

Otha composed herself. She sat a little straighter in her chair, trying to draw optimism and strength from the gentle warmth of the sunbeam. Grip, sensing her anxiety, fluttered over from his favorite brillbane perch to settle on his preferred spot on the back of her right hand. He glanced up, his black eyes shrewd and a little worried.

The tessila's scales were still as brilliant a purple as ever, but he, too, was showing signs of age. Several scales along his brow ridge had shed out only to grow in flat black instead of incandescent purple. These days, Grip never ventured far from Otha's side. Being apart made both of them anxious.

More murmuring drifted in from the hall. Willis appeared, looking flustered as usual. "High Mage Agina will see you now, if you're ready, my lady."

Otha waved a thin hand and the young man withdrew. Otha closed her eyes. Grip settled down, shifting his stiff joints so his soft belly was snugged up against her worn skin.

There was the tap of shoes and the rustling of fabric as Agina entered and settled into the chair opposite Otha. For a moment, Otha considered keeping her eyes closed – letting them think she'd drifted off to sleep. They all thought her half senile anyway. She wasn't, of course. She just found it increasingly difficult to care about the mundane conflicts they so often brought to her to resolve.

But she knew why Agina had come today. She also knew the other woman wouldn't leave until they'd spoken. With tired reluctance, she opened her eyes.

The High Mage sat upright and rigid in her chair. Her tessila, Fara, sat on her knee, wings tucked back and chin held aloft. They'd both always been a bit proud. But then, who was Otha to cast that particular stone?

"Hello, Agina," Otha said. Although Otha's skin was thin and her eyes watery, her voice was still strong. She was glad of that. It wouldn't do for the First Mage to speak in wavering tones.

Agina didn't waste time with pleasantries. She rarely did. "We have authorized a party to leave the valley. They will collect intelligence regarding the current state of affairs at Tessili Academy, and infiltrate the court. We need to know more about public sentiment in the current culture to make informed decisions."

Otha said nothing. Grip settled a little lower on her hand, growing drowsy. Otha could remember a time he'd have bristled just at having another tessila in his territory. She supposed age had mellowed them both.

There was a long silence. Outside, a breeze was blowing the tops of the pine trees, making them wave and bend in fitful bobs. In the greenhouse, all was still.

Agina shifted, and continued. "It's our hope there might be less fear in the populace now. So much time has passed since the Betrayal."

Beyond the pine trees, the mountains reared. From her vantage, Otha could only see their snow-blanketed shoulders. The peaks, she knew, reached high into the bright sky – jagged tops raking at the heavens. At their base hung the mists, thick and heavy. Otha could feel them, the trickle of thought and energy that spell took from her. She'd been helping to hold the mists in place since the day they'd been summoned.

She understood the hope that drove the younger people to search for a way out. She couldn't deny the Tessilari were slowly dying in this place. When they'd settled here, everyone had feared the population would outgrow this valley. Now, houses stood abandoned at the ends of streets. In the 384 years since the remnants of the Tessilari had found refuge in this place, the tessili they'd brought with them had thrived briefly, then begun to fail. And so the Tessilari failed as well.

Otha understood the hope, yes, but she didn't share it. She closed her eyes again, feeling the vast loneliness that came with an unusually long life. She was the only living Tessilari who remembered – who had seen the people of Masidon go mad. She'd seen the men and women who'd fought beside her in the long, brutal War of the Diods turn the weapons the Tessilari had created for use against a common enemy back on those who had made them. So much of her long life had faded in her mind—the faces of her loved ones, the tenor of her own mother's voice—but she remembered those terrible days when man had fought man, brother had betrayed brother, and, at last, the Tessilari had fled.

So she understood High Mage Agina's reasons for pushing. She even sympathized. But she couldn't agree with the decision. She met the younger woman's sharp gaze. It was the curse of the old, to know so much and be so little regarded. Oh, they pretended to respect her. But they no longer heeded what she said.

First Mage Otha did the only thing she could do. She repeated what she'd been saying for centuries. She spoke with the conviction only one granted the sight could claim when speaking about the future. "Our moment will come," she said. "If we wait."

High Mage Agina's lips compressed in an expression of frustration. She didn't understand. She didn't truly believe in the sight, just as a man without hearing cannot believe in music. First Mage Otha was the last of the Tessilari who possessed this particular gift. There was no one left who understood her.

Agina let out a slow breath, and stood. She was disappointed. Well, so was Otha. The First Mage responded with only the barest of nods as the younger woman took her leave and walked out of the room.

Otha settled back onto her cushions. She closed her eyes. She wasn't trying to *see*, but she did anyway. A face rose up behind her eyes. It was a face as familiar as even her own, so often she'd seen it. And it was not a nice face.

Eyes closed, sun warm on her skin, Otha *saw* what she'd seen so many times in her 403 years of life. She saw the man, face twisted into a scowl, walking with a pronounced limp, leading the thin, grubby child on a leash towards ….

She could never see what. She could never see why. She could never see when.

Such were the limitations of the sight. She only knew this man, whoever he was, would deliver their moment. If only the Tessilari would wait.

◈

Jey swung her staff at Treyam's head, keeping her balance distributed between her two feet. As she expected, Treyam stepped back. In the moment of his movement, she ducked, let go of one end of the staff, and sent a ferocious swipe towards his knees. Just for practice, she knit a quick active force spell and dropped it onto the staff. She felt the velocity of her swing increase.

The staff, carved all over in a filigree of ancient runes, hummed with magic. It was an ancient weapon, beautifully crafted. The stone it had been made from somehow altered to be hard as iron, light as bamboo, and very receptive to magic. She'd discovered how to make it burn in her hands, how to back it up with deadly force, and how to call it to her from as far away as she could get. The staff was the sort of thing Jey had hoped to find in the Valley of Mist when she'd first arrived.

Unfortunately, it was not hers. The staff belonged to Treyam. There were only six such weapons in the valley. Treyam had inherited his from his father, who had been given it by his father before him. It was a treasured and revered artifact of a time when the Tessilari had been a different sort of people.

Jey had no hope of getting one of her own. The art of making such things was lost.

The staff, fortunately, was also enchanted so it could not harm one of its own blood. Still, Jey had not learned to trust the thing entirely. Even while her heart beat a little faster and her blood pounded in her veins, adrenaline singing in her system as she imagined the blow that swing would have delivered had it been leveled against a true opponent, she pulled the staff at the last moment and only tapped lightly on Treyam's knees.

The young man collapsed into the grass anyway, laughing in mock defeat. Jey straightened, setting the end of the staff on the ground. For a moment, irritation overtook all other emotion. She stared down at Treyam. His warm brown eyes were alight, his skin flushed with exertion. He'd dropped the weapon he'd been using – Jey's staff, which was made of fine hardwood but no match for the one Treyam loaned her with increasing frequency. *This is the problem*, she thought as she stared down, feeling the frustrated tension in her shoulders, the tightness of her jaw. *They don't take it seriously.*

If Treyam sensed her disapproval, he gave no sign. His laughter smoothed into his trademark half grin. He stretched to his full length on the smooth lawn. It was a fine day. Although the edge never seemed to leave the wind here in this high valley, today the sun was warm.

Jey found herself softening against her will. How could she blame them, really? She lifted her eyes to the jagged mountains that surrounded them, peaks reaching towards the sky like broken teeth, ringing them in on all sides. The fog lay at their base. For centuries, the Tessilari had lived with a twofold defense against reality.

In an absent gesture, Jey rubbed a hand over the inside of her elbow. Concealed there, beneath her sleeve, were the scars. There were hundreds of them – pale pricks in her skin where the needle had gone in, again and again. *I will not forget.* She made this promise to herself every day. She made it for the same reason she insisted Treyam spar with her every day. She made it because it would be so easy to let things slip. And Jey had already forgotten enough for a lifetime.

She shivered, the sweat on her brow cooling. She felt a brief stab of loneliness for Phril. He was fine, she knew. He was in one of the greenhouses, basking in the sun, stretched out on a brillbane leaf. It was too cold for the plants and tessili alike outside of the greenhouses. At first, Phril hadn't liked to be separated from her. He'd refused to stay behind. But here in the Valley of Mist, his wings grew stiff in the knife-edged air. Slowly he'd become accustomed to letting her leave him. She could feel him growing more and more complacent by the day.

On the one hand, she was glad. It had alarmed her when she'd learned other tessili could be reasonable – that they could think rationally and adjust their behavior accordingly to logic. Phril had never possessed that skill. He'd always been volatile, often behaving in ways that could easily have led to his own death, and thus Jey's as well. Seeing him change now that their lives were not in danger gave Jey hope for his sanity.

Still, she missed him a little.

Nine months, Jey had been here. She knew she'd lost her edge. Phril was going soft, Elle wasn't even trying to maintain her combat skills. The restless frustration boiled up in Jey again as she turned to stare at the mouth of the valley, where a narrow gap in the mountains stood blocked by the heavy mist.

There was a rustle of fabric as Treyam rose. He took a moment to brush the clinging grass from his sleeves. He came to Jey and stood next to her, following her gaze.

As so often happened, Jey felt a little tug of … something … when Treyam came near. He stood beside her now, his body blocking the breeze. She was aware of how close he was, how easily he could reach out and touch her.

Jey took a small step away, as she always did when she felt that tug. It wasn't that she didn't want to respond, or that she wasn't curious about where the pull might lead her. But she could see what falling in love with Lokim had done to Elle. It was another temptation Jey had to resist if she had any hope of doing what she'd promised.

The Academy still stood out there, far down in the valley of Deramor. And Jey would not let her attention be diverted until the men who had made those scars on her arm were brought to justice.

As if reading her thoughts, Treyam spoke. "Tomorrow." His voice was smooth and rich. He spoke now in a low tone, barely loud enough to hear. "Tomorrow, at last," he said, "they will let me fulfill my promise to you."

About the Author

Robin has always been enamored with magic.

When she was a child, that meant reading books. When she was a slightly older child, it meant trying to write her own. She produced her first attempt at a fantasy story at the age of 10. It was an unintentionally blatant (and considerably less well executed) rip-off of *The Lion, the Witch, and the Wardrobe*.

Fortunately for everyone, Robin's stories have gotten a little more original over the years. She currently lives in Iowa City, where she hangs out with her husband, trains horses, and writes.

learn more at robinstephen.com

Robin also writes contemporary western romance

If you like horses, love stories, and the desert, explore Robin's work under the pen name Stefani Wilder. Her book, *A Man Who Rides* is available now.

see stefaniwilder.com for details